A PARASITE IN THE MIN

A PARASITE
IN THE MIND

A Journey through the Dark Boroughs of a Paedophilic Cannibal's Mind

Eat the Evidence: Part Two

John C. Espy

KARNAC

First published in 2015 by
Karnac Books Ltd
118 Finchley Road
London NW3 5HT

British Library Cataloguing in Publication Data

A C.I.P. for this book is available from the British Library

ISBN-13: 978-1-78220-092-5

Typeset by V Publishing Solutions Pvt Ltd., Chennai, India

Printed in Great Britain

www.karnacbooks.com

For Treasa Glinnwater

PREFACE

The first volume of *Eat The Evidence* told the story of Nathaneal Bar Jonah coming into being and his ascension to pedophilic proficiency by mastering the art of what one might call the *penetrant puppeteer*: one who takes on the characteristics of a large nematocyst that adroitly threads a barb into the body of its prey to inject its toxin and paralyze its victim. The second volume, *A Parasite In The Mind*, takes the reader deeper into the perpetrator's reign of terror and his devastating effect on the three young boys that Bar Jonah marked as prey just as Part One ended. It also tells of how those boys would ultimately prove to be Bar Jonah's undoing. A third volume will follow.

John Espy

CHAPTER ONE

"The best-laid schemes go oft awry"

Zach had the Good Guy Breakfast coming up and Doc had promised to go with him. He was going to go as the boy's grandfather. His best friend. Zach wanted Doc to wear his red fuzzy hat. But that morning when Zach arrived at Doc's, Doc planned to tell him they had to leave for Canada right then. Doc would already have everything packed up and ready to go. Zach was just going to have to understand. In life you can't have everything you want. Some things just have to be sacrificed for love.

Zach had told Doc that Rachel was in a tizzy about Carl getting ready to move out. All they did was fight, Zach had said. Doc told Bar Jonah goodbye the night before he planned to leave. Bar Jonah could have whatever he wanted from Doc's place for his toy business. He had been such a good friend. Doc knew Bar Jonah would give his many toy friends a good home. It would be Doc's parting gift to Bar Jonah. Because of Zach, Doc was getting the opportunity a man of his age rarely gets, the chance to start his life anew. Zach said he wanted to let Rachel know where he was once they got to Canada. Doc assured him that would be okay. He would even help Zach write every letter

1

to Rachel and then take them to the mailbox for him. Doc also told Zach he shouldn't be disappointed if Rachel didn't write him back for a long time, because she may get pretty mad that he had gone so far away. That was okay, Zach had said, because Rachel never knew where he was anyway.

Doc, with a quivering voice, told Bar Jonah that Zach had helped him concentrate all of the meaning of his life into one point of light. Zach had allowed Doc to resolve the riddle of his existence that had been weighing on him so painfully of late. It seemed that with each year of getting agonizingly older, Doc became consumed with more and more inescapable angst about being alone. With Zach however, Doc said he would not have to die by himself. When Bar Jonah realized that Doc was serious about taking Zach away, he bored deeply into Doc's eyes and said Zach wasn't going anywhere. He had not finished with Zach yet.

While Doc was waiting for Zach that morning, he prepared a special cup of hot cocoa that would help Zach sleep when they first began their journey. He would time it just right and help Zach walk to the car just before he fell sound asleep. This way he wouldn't have to carry him, which he didn't even know if he could; Zach was a big boy. By the time Zach woke up they'd be across the border.

* * *

Doc despised Bar Jonah for his meanness. But like everything else that had happened in his life, several stiff drinks helped Doc make believe that whatever had caused him so much torment, simply had never happened.

Bar Jonah sympathized with Doc and told him how sorry he felt that Doc had lost another opportunity for love. He understood; it was a sad destiny for men like them. He knew how much Zach had meant to Doc. That was why Bar Jonah said he wanted to bring so much pleasure into Doc's life now; to give some of Zach back to Doc. Bar Jonah would often put his arm around Doc's shoulder and tell him he deserved as much pleasure as he could find in the final years of his life. Secretly though, the only question for Bar Jonah was how to cleanse himself of the humiliation that Doc had wantonly decided to spew all over him when he had lured Zach into his lair with hot cocoa on those snowy mornings. Bar Jonah knew that making Zach disappear would cause Doc immeasurable suffering until the day he died of a broken heart, while bringing Bar Jonah deliverance from the tormenting jealousy he felt for Doc.

In the days after losing Zach, Doc would sit on a butt-worn stool at the HiHo, draw deeply on his cigarette, throw back a shot or two of sour mash whiskey and stare back at himself in the faulted, murky mirror hanging above the bar. Doc's seductive, red rheumy eyes, lurking behind his resin glasses, bore the lines of the inescapable suffering that now lived in the core of his being at the loss of Zach. He was plagued by reruns of the morning that he anxiously waited at the door with his heart a flutter, for Zach to come to him. It would have been so luscious, so delightful, so fulfilling to close out his life so enslaved by such other-worldly bliss. But as the hands on the clock ticked by so painfully slow, Doc realized that Zach would never be coming to him. Then he would stumble to the door, make his way home and fall onto the cold, cat piss stained linoleum floor and begin to sob uncontrollably.

Proclaiming harsh judgments

A tumultuous river scene painted on heavy cardboard hung above Bar Jonah's couch. He had put the painting there, in all of its darkness, as a constant reminder to the three boys of God's ever-present wrath, seething and vengeful, waiting to explode when children didn't do as they were told. Bar Jonah would explain that in the painting, along the mossy bank of the Lord's river, grew a burning bush. Its soft ember glow was ready to ignite and set ablaze any child who resisted being guided along the path of redemption. Etched into the cardboard canvas was a foreboding black and blue sky. Bar Jonah told the boys that the sky represented the story of Abraham, whom the Lord called upon to sacrifice his own son Isaac, in order to prove that he loved the Lord above all others. The boys would stand transfixed with dread when Bar Jonah called for them to come together in front of the painting. Bar Jonah like to say their special time in front of the painting was "church". Sometimes Bar Jonah would even put pants on and snuff out his cigarette before church, saying it was more respectful. Bar Jonah offered up his interpretation of the painting every time he presided over their church service. He even read verses from his Bible, much of which he said he had translated himself from the original Hebrew. He especially liked reading to the boys from the book of Leviticus. Children *were* the lambs of God, Leviticus would say. Good children obeyed the ones who loved and cared for them *without* question. Children who refused to obey suffered the fate of being consumed by the rushing waters or burned by the torrid flames. When dark clouds appeared overhead, God was calling upon the Shepherd who loved children to bring them to Him in sacrifice. The only way the good Shepherd could resist God's calling was if the children had done what they had been told. Otherwise, the Shepherd would not be able to resist God's command to kill them.

Set design

One afternoon, a few months after the boys became a regular part of Bar Jonah's life, they came down to find a beige sheet hanging over the entrance to Bar Jonah's tiny dining room. Stormy wanted to know what the sheet was hiding. It had to be a secret. Bar Jonah told him to stay the hell away. It was none of his business. They were always getting into his things. Stormy kept running up and trying to pull out the thumbtacks that held the sheet tightly pinned against the edge of the wall.

4

Bar Jonah would scream that it wasn't a fucking joke and yell for Stormy to stop.

Stormy thought Bar Jonah was kidding around again. Roland told Stormy to stop too. He could see that Bar Jonah was getting more and more worked up. Stormy ran up to Bar Jonah, jumped on his lap and said he was sorry. Bar Jonah told him it was all right. Stormy put his head on Bar Jonah's shoulder and nestled his cheek against Bar Jonah's ear. Bar Jonah pulled him close. Then Stormy suddenly screamed, "KIDDING" right into Bar Jonah's ear. Bar Jonah threw Stormy onto the floor. Stormy jumped up and ran toward the sheet, got a hold of one of the edges and pulled hard. Several of the thumbtacks popped out of the wall and a corner flap of the sheet hung loose. Bar Jonah jumped up from the couch and called Stormy a little bastard, grabbing Stormy by the shoulder and throwing him against the couch, screaming that he was going to fucking kill him. Stormy hit the edge of the couch and feigned that his leg was hurt. Then he rolled up onto the couch, laid back and pulled his left leg up to his chest, whimpering. Bar Jonah turned around and slammed his right foot into the wall, causing the cheap plasterboard wall to spew white dust when he pulled his foot out of the hole. Bar Jonah picked up the thumb tacks off of the floor, took the flap of the curtain between his fingers and pushed the tacks back through the sheet into the wall. Then Bar Jonah turned around and walked over to Stormy. Stormy was lying shaking on the couch. Roland had jumped up from Bar Jonah's recliner and started walking toward the couch, thinking that Bar Jonah was going to kill Stormy. Bar Jonah glared at Roland, freezing him in his steps with his eyes, telling him to stay back. Roland stopped and sat back down in the recliner. Bar Jonah was breathing hard, hovering above Stormy. He picked Stormy up and pulled him against his chest. Bar Jonah whispered into Stormy's ear that he wasn't going to hurt him. He just wanted him to mind and to stay away from the sheet. Stormy melded into Bar Jonah's arms softly sobbing, saying he was really sorry this time and he would never be bad again. Bar Jonah told him he knew he wouldn't and not to worry about the wall that he had kicked. He was going to help Stormy fix it. Bar Jonah sat back down on the couch and held Stormy until he stopped crying. Then he told Roland to take Stormy back upstairs. He had some things he needed to do.

* * *

A few hours later Roland came back downstairs and tearfully told Bar Jonah he needed to talk to him. Bar Jonah wasn't being as nice as he used to be, Roland sniveled. He always seemed grumpy now and didn't want to spend as much time with him as he did before. Then Roland turned bashfully away, facing the kitchen with his chin resting on his chest.

Bar Jonah sighed and lit a cigarette, blew the smoke out of his nose and told him that wasn't true. He loved them more than their parents. There was just a lot on his mind. A few minutes later, Bar Jonah pushed his cigarette through a chrome, spring-loaded circular trap door, into a metal ashtray covered in red leather. A tiny whiff of smoke escaped just as the spring popped the trap door closed. Then Bar Jonah tip-toed up behind Roland.

Roland felt Bar Jonah's arms wrap around him and wrestle him to the ground, rolling around on top of him, laughing and being silly. Bar Jonah pinched Roland on the butt and told him they should go into the bedroom and wrestle on the bed, make up, and then take a nap. Roland squirmed out from underneath Bar Jonah and ran down the hallway, through the bedroom door and jumped onto the bed. Bar Jonah was chasing right behind. Bar Jonah pulled his shirt over his head and flopped onto bed with Roland. He reached out and pulled Roland against him and said he was sorry for ignoring him and getting so mad at Stormy. He didn't mean to make Roland think he didn't love them. Bar Jonah said the boys, especially

Roland, were the kids he never had. Roland got tears in his eyes, put his head on Bar Jonah's chest and fell asleep.

Would-be troublemaker

Adam Kingsland had met Barry in grade school, but they didn't start becoming friends until junior high. He couldn't understand why Barry lived with Bar Jonah, but figured it must be because Bar Jonah only charged him a $100 a month. Pretty cheap Barry would say. Kingsland also knew Bar Jonah a bit from Hardee's and like everyone else at the restaurant, he couldn't stand him.

Kingsland sometimes went over to Bar Jonah's apartment to play Monopoly with Barry. But as soon as Bar Jonah came into the room where he and Barry were playing, Kingsland felt his skin begin to crawl. Then Kingsland always wanted to end the game pretty fast, even if he had to lose. Barry would tell him to sit down and stop acting like a pussy.

The smell in the apartment made Kingsland gag. He asked Barry how he could stand to live in a place that smelled so bad. Kingsland didn't think Barry ever gave him a very good answer. A couple of times Kingsland even tried to stay over with Barry, but he would wake up around four, tossing and turning because the smell seemed to come out more at night and pervade every square inch of the apartment. There was no way to get away from it. Kingsland also told Barry he thought it was strange that Bar Jonah ran around just in his briefs with kids around. Barry agreed and said he had told Bar Jonah that he was going to get into trouble. It worried Barry because Bar Jonah sometimes slept with the kids too. However, their mother knew what was going on and she didn't seem to give much of a shit. Why should he? The last time Kingsland was at the apartment he asked Barry why there was a sheet covering the area where the kitchen table sat. Barry said he didn't know,

Bar Jonah had put it up the day before. He had just come home from work and found it draped over the archway.

Barry suggested they watch some television and that he would make some popcorn. As they were standing by the stove talking about what to watch, Barry suddenly cocked his head up, wrinkled his nose and sniffed a couple of times, before he realized that smoke was pushing out from between the kernels of burning popcorn. He hadn't put enough oil into the thin-bottomed pan and had turned the burner all the way up. Barry picked up the smoking pan and sat it down in the sink. Some of the kernels were still popping wildly out of the pan. Barry started acting silly, flapping his hands through the manic kernels, sending several of the hot disobedient maize husks bouncing off of the tile wall behind the sink. Barry laughed and yelled to Kingsland he was being attacked by an army of kernels.

After Barry cleaned up the mess he had made in the kitchen, he and Kingsland finally sat down to watch some television. Kingsland was distracted though. His eyes seemed to be continuously drawn over to the sheet. Barry asked Kingsland where he was going, as he started to push himself up against the torn and tattered arms of the couch. Kingsland said he was going to look behind the sheet. Barry told him to sit back down and leave well enough alone. It would piss Bar Jonah off if he found out that the sheet had been messed with. The springs in the couch were sprung from so much weight and bouncing that Kingsland felt his butt being grasped in the clutches of the cushions, when he followed Barry's command to sit back down. Before the movie was over, Kingsland told Barry he was going to leave and not come back anymore.

* * *

A couple of days later, Kingsland discovered he had lost his ID badge. He had probably left it at Bar Jonah's, Kingsland thought. He drove over to Bar Jonah's and knocked on the door. When the door opened, Kingsland saw Bar Jonah standing naked, except for his jockey shorts. Kingsland told Bar Jonah he thought he had left his ID badge there. Bar Jonah told him he could come in and look for it. Bar Jonah stepped aside and let Kingsland come inside. Kingsland walked over to the couch, leaned down and ran his fingers around the edge of the cushions, where he felt the stiff plastic lip of his ID. Kingsland gripped the badge between his thumb and forefinger, pulled it up from between the cushions and slipped it into his pocket, saying out loud that he had found it. Bar Jonah had just stood by watching. When Kingsland straightened back up, Bar Jonah seductively cocked his hip, looked at him and asked if he needed anything else. Kingsland said no and walked toward the door. As Kingsland was closing the apartment door behind him, he looked around and saw Bar Jonah still standing in the same spot. His feet hadn't moved, but Bar Jonah had pivoted his head around and was glaring somehow defiantly at Kingsland. Kingsland, confused, pulled the door closed, went to his car and drove around for a while, shaking his head and deciding that no matter what, he would never again go back to Bar Jonah's.

Nosey

A few days later, Barry had heard Bar Jonah doing some drilling behind the sheet. That surprised him, because Bar Jonah didn't seem like he would know which end of a drill to use. Later that afternoon, after Bar Jonah had taken the boys to a matinee, Barry, sitting on the couch, decided it was time to know what Bar Jonah had been doing behind the sheet. If he didn't want any of Bar Jonah's antics to cause him any problems, then he had to know what Bar Jonah had been up to. Barry got up, walked over and looked defiantly at the sheet. He stood hesitant. Barry remembered Bar Jonah walking past him saying "Do not touch the sheet," taunting Barry with

9

curiosity. Barry shook his head and thought of how stupid he felt sometimes for being so compliant with Bar Jonah's orders.

Barry reached up and with a butter knife pried out two thumbtacks that were holding a small section of sheet against the wall. A flap gapped open when the tension on the sheet was let loose. Barry pulled the sheet back, stuck his head through the small opening and peered behind the drape. Lying on the kitchen table, Barry saw an old paint-splattered drill with a fat bit locked in its chuck. There was also a brand new orange stud finder, with a tiny blinking red light. Barry turned his head from side to side and didn't see any obvious holes in the walls. But he knew he had heard Bar Jonah drilling just a few days before. Then Barry looked up. A one-inch diameter hole had been drilled through the ceiling and into the stud right above the kitchen table. Screwed into the stud was a small pulley. When Barry saw the pulley, he decided he didn't want to know any more. He pulled his head out of the opening and pushed the thumbtacks back through the same holes he had pulled them out of. Then he left the apartment and drove around for a while smoking dope. When Barry pulled back into the parking lot, he saw Bar Jonah's car parked up on the sidewalk that divided the parking lot from the apartment building. The manager had told Bar Jonah over and over again not to park on the sidewalk. Bar Jonah protested, saying he had a bad back because of his weight. The closer he could get to his apartment door, the less his back hurt. If the apartment manager had any problems with Bar Jonah's disability, he could take it up with his attorney. When Barry went into the apartment, he saw the sheet had been taken down and the drill and stud finder were nowhere to be seen. Bar Jonah had even emptied the always-overflowing skull and crossbones ashtray that sat on the kitchen table. Now the pulley dangled prominently from the stud in the ceiling.

CHAPTER TWO

Trojan Horse of compassion

Bar Jonah knocked on Lori's door. When Lori answered, she
saw Bar Jonah standing with his arms outstretched, holding
a large bowl of coleslaw. Lori thanked him for the food and
started to shut the door. Bar Jonah insisted on coming in. He
wanted to talk to Lori about the boys. They're starting to lie,
Bar Jonah said. He had caught them in several lies recently and
he was worried about why such good boys would be lying.
Sure, they were rambunctious at times, but they were a lot of
fun, especially for a man who had not had kids of his own.
They made him feel like a real dad. Lori said she thought they
were having a hard time at school. There was a lot of racism in
the schools and the other kids were probably picking on them
because they were Indians. Bar Jonah said that was probably
what was wrong. He just wanted Lori to know he was worried
because lying can be a sign that something is not right at home.
Bar Jonah said he knew Lori was out a lot at night and Gerald
was either at work or sleeping. So he would be sure and give
the boys extra attention to help Lori and Gerald out. He would
let her know if the boys started telling bigger fibs. Lori told Bar
Jonah she had noticed Roland being quieter than usual; she

had wondered if something was wrong too. Bar Jonah said he had noticed that too. He had only caught Roland in a couple of small lies, but Bar Jonah was still worried. Stormy was lying a lot. Bar Jonah couldn't think of any specific examples but it really didn't matter. He just wanted to let Lori know he was worried. Lori did say that Stormy's teacher had called from school, because Stormy was saying bad words in class. The teacher said she'd heard Stormy making a lot of jokes about his wiener and his butt. Bar Jonah said he'd keep an eye out for that too. He agreed with Lori that there was a lot of racism at the school. The teachers treated the Indian kids real different. They made a lot of cracks to the Indian kids that white kids didn't have to put up with. Bar Jonah knew about being discriminated against because he was fat as a kid. The teachers and the other kids had picked on him too. Then Bar Jonah hung his head and shamefully said he needed to get something off of his chest. He had never told anyone about it before. With wet eyes he told Lori about being brutally raped as a young boy. That was what had caused him to get involved in doing undercover work for the police at the schools. Lori said she was sorry that Bar Jonah had had so many bad things happen to him. He didn't deserve that, she said. Bar Jonah told Lori he knew what really went on in the schools that the parents wouldn't ever find out about. He thanked Lori for being such a good mom to the boys. Bar Jonah said he had a real good mom too, the best. Good moms stand by you when no one else would. When Bar Jonah started to leave, Lori put her arms around him and hugged him close. Bar Jonah hugged her back. If she weren't already married, she'd be thinking about hooking up with him, Lori said. Bar Jonah said he felt the same way about her too. After Bar Jonah left, Lori took the coleslaw into the kitchen and dumped it into the trash. Bar Jonah was a real good man, but she wouldn't eat anything he cooked unless it came from a package. Everything he made had a funny taste. She had told her boys not to eat anything Bar Jonah made either, unless they saw him take it out of a store-bought package. Sometimes when she and the boys were down at Bar Jonah's, he would get some deer meat out of his freezer and put it in a sink of hot water to thaw it out. He said he was going to make his special deer burgers for everyone. Lori always tried to make up some kind of excuse and grab the boys and take them upstairs. Sometimes when she couldn't think of any reason to leave, they had to stay and eat. More than anything she didn't want to make Bar Jonah angry.

* * *

Roland was now at Bar Jonah's so much, it was almost like he was living there. Bar Jonah even joked with Roland about just going ahead and moving in. If he did, they could have a lot more fun. They could even take trips together. Bar Jonah said he used to take trips with another kid who'd been a special friend. But the kid's mother never knew they had been so close. Roland asked where his friend was now. "In heaven," Bar Jonah replied.

Lori thought it'd be a good idea for Roland to stay with Bar Jonah too. Gerald didn't have any time for Roland with working so much and she was gone all the time. It was clear that Roland needed a dad now more than ever, with all of the questions he had started asking about sex and everything.

Roland talked to Stormy and Stanley and told them he was going to stay with Bar Jonah for a while to see how it worked out. Stormy and Stanley yelled and screamed that it wasn't fair. They should get to stay too. Roland told them to shut up; they were just kids. He was fourteen. Bar Jonah called Doc as soon as he had the idea about Roland moving in. Doc could barely contain his jealousy. If Stormy and Stanley wanted to move in with him, he would certainly welcome them with open arms. He would even be glad to meet with Lori and extend the offer himself. She wouldn't even have to pay for food. They seemed like such nice boys. Doc said he thought it would be comforting to Lori knowing that her boys were living not only with a doctor but also a child psychologist. He could take care of their physical needs and understand their minds, all at the same time.

* * *

Bar Jonah got pissed at Doc and told him to stay away from Stormy and Stanley. Doc said he wasn't able to get out and meet boys like he used to. It was getting to the point where he actually needed his cane in order to walk. It wasn't just for show any more. Bar Jonah was a selfish bastard, Doc thought. He was going to have a live-in chattel and wasn't willing to share his good fortune. Bar Jonah told Doc he loved Roland. He was helping to raise him. Lori couldn't do it by herself and Gerald was never around. Bar Jonah was picking up the slack. He was now spending more time with the boys than either Lori or Gerald, especially with Roland. Doc also told Bar Jonah to get rid of Barry. "He is going to be a problem, you wait and see," Doc said. Bar Jonah said he could take care of Barry.

* * *

The first day of March was blustery and cold. Lori was getting tired of being pestered by Bar Jonah. "Let Roland come and stay with me," he kept hounding. Finally, Lori agreed. Roland was looking forward to going places and getting to do more things. Lori was looking forward to having one less kid to worry about. Roland didn't have many clothes to take down to Bar Jonah's. Mainly a couple of pairs of sweats, canvas high-top sneakers from a local discount store that were stretched out and flopped around on his feet from never being laced up, a few tee shirts and underwear. Bar Jonah had enough fun things around the apartment so that Roland didn't have to bring anything like that. Just his clothes, Bar Jonah had said. The first night Roland was there, he slept on the couch. His clothes were stuffed into a plastic bag from the local market. Just like at home, he would root around and find what he needed to wear for the day. The next morning, Roland decided he didn't want to go to school. He wasn't learning that much anyway. Bar Jonah said instead, they would go out to lunch to celebrate Roland moving in. Bar Jonah left early that morning, starting his day with his usual cigarettes and coffee. Roland liked coffee too, but Bar Jonah's coffee was so strong he couldn't drink it. Bar Jonah set the timer on the coffee maker for three a.m. He had measured out the coffee and the water the night before and the coffee started brewing when the timer went off. This way the coffee would set for several hours and thicken up. Bar Jonah said his morning *motor oil* helped him to get going.

When Roland woke up the next morning, he pulled on his sweats and tee shirt but didn't bother changing his underwear. He wasn't going to eat a lot for breakfast, because they were going to have a big lunch. Roland looked into the kitchen and saw Bar Jonah getting his coffee mug ready. He never did this unless he was going to be gone for the day. Roland hadn't realized they were going to have fun for the whole day. He asked Bar Jonah where they were going. Bar Jonah turned around, pulled his cigarette out of his mouth and said he was driving up to Canada for the day. He told Roland to stay in the apartment and clean the place up. It was a mess. Bar Jonah walked out of the apartment, slamming the door behind him. Roland puttered around the apartment most of the day, moving things around, but never picking up a rag to clean anything.

About eight, Bar Jonah's rusty muffler let Roland know he was home. He was expecting him to come right on inside, but instead Roland heard Bar Jonah walking up the stairs to Lori's. In a few minutes Bar Jonah opened the apartment door followed by Stanley. Roland asked Bar Jonah why Stanley was there. Bar Jonah said he was going to spend the night with him. Roland said there wasn't any place for Stanley to sleep. He already had dibs on the couch. Bar Jonah looked at Stanley and told him he could sleep in his bed. Roland went over to the couch and with a pout plopped down on the plush lion throw he had been using for a blanket. Bar Jonah sarcastically told Roland to stop sulking.

"Come here," Bar Jonah said to Roland. Roland walked over to Bar Jonah, who told him to lean against the wall. He was going to teach him how to put handcuffs on someone. First Bar Jonah was going to handcuff Roland. Then he was going to have Roland handcuff Stanley. Bar Jonah was also going to teach them how to assume the position, so they could be patted down. "Lean face forward into the wall," Bar Jonah said. He called Stanley over to watch, so he could teach him too. He had a lot of experience cuffing suspects with the U.S. Marshals.

Roland felt Bar Jonah grab his arms by the wrist and twist them behind his back. Bar Jonah held Roland's arms tightly and slapped the edge of the cuffs hard against Roland's wrists as though he were resisting. Roland started breathing faster when he heard the rapid, small clicks of the stainless restraints locking into place. Bar Jonah stepped back, looked at Stanley and commented how easy it was. Anyone can learn how to do it. Roland felt Bar Jonah's fist curled up in the middle of his back, holding him against the wall. Bar Jonah said it didn't take any effort once someone is handcuffed to control them. "If you take away the use of their arms, most people forget how to use their feet. The most they're going to do is fall down and flop around. If they do, you can just start kicking them in the head."

Bar Jonah told Stanley to step up and press his fist into Roland's back. Stanley only weighed about one hundred and fifty pounds. Roland was twice that. Stanley walked up behind Roland. Instead of pushing his fist into Roland's back like Bar Jonah was doing, Stanley swung his fist and punched Roland in between his shoulder—blades. Roland's shoulders doubled inward as he cried out in pain. With his face pressed into the wall, Roland told Bar Jonah to take the cuffs off and started to turn around. Bar Jonah took his right foot and put it between Roland's spread feet. Bar Jonah then swiftly swept his foot from left to right, kicking Roland's ankles, causing Roland to have to use the wall to balance himself. Roland started crying. Bar Jonah grabbed Roland by the hair and pressed him hard against the plaster wall, still pushing on one ankle, so he couldn't balance. Stanley called Roland a pussy. Bar Jonah told Roland as soon as he stopped sniveling he would take the handcuffs off. Roland sucked up his snot and tried to sound like he wasn't crying anymore. Bar Jonah let go of his head and moved his right foot, taking the pressure off of Roland's ankle, letting him stand up straight. Roland started twisting his wrists in a panic, wanting to be set free as Bar Jonah was fumbling with the tiny ankh-shaped key. Bar Jonah wrapped his hand around the metal links that connected the bracelets and torqued the cuffs in an upward motion. The handcuffs cut into Roland's wrist bone causing a droplet of blood to form and tears to well up in Roland's eyes again. Bar Jonah yelled at Roland, telling him to stand fucking still. In a few seconds, Roland felt the cuffs fall away from his wrist when Bar Jonah finally managed to turn the spring release with the key.

Roland then shoved himself off of the wall and grabbed Stanley by the nape of the neck, turned him around to face the wall and tried to grab the handcuffs out of Bar Jonah's hand. Now it was Stanley's turn. Bar Jonah wouldn't give the cuffs to Roland. Roland held Stanley by the nape of the neck, dragging his face across the sharp pocked drywall, as he now used his weight to control him. Stanley, in a muffled scream, yelled that Roland was hurting him. Roland screamed, "Fuck you," asking him how *he* liked it. "Don't you ever fucking laugh at me," Roland screamed again. Stanley started crying when Roland grabbed his arms and twisted them hard behind his back. Roland again reached over and tried to take the cuffs out of Bar Jonah's hands. Bar Jonah held them tight. He said no. Roland felt Bar Jonah's short, strong fingers pry his hands away from Stanley's neck. Go and sit down, he said. They had done enough training for one night.

Bar Jonah then put his arm around Stanley and pulled him close, caressing the back of his neck and head, asking him if Roland had hurt him. Roland had gone over to the couch, and sat down with his head in his hands, blubbering. Bar Jonah told Stanley they should go on to bed. It was getting late; he would rub his neck where Roland had hurt him in bed. Roland saw Bar Jonah and Stanley walk down the hallway and go into Bar Jonah's room. Then he saw the bedroom door close. A few minutes later Roland, still sobbing on the couch, heard Stanley giggling, telling Bar Jonah to stop tickling him. Roland curled up and pulled the lion throw over his head and cried himself to sleep.

* * *

The next morning, Roland smelled Bar Jonah's cigarette, before he saw the profile of his head, pulling back the curtains, peering out the living room window. A few minutes later, he saw Stanley walking down the hallway in his briefs. Bar Jonah walked over to the couch and rubbed Roland on the head. They were going to spend the day together and go to the movies later on. Bar Jonah told Roland to decide what he wanted to see. It didn't matter how he had acted the night before, Bar Jonah forgave him. After he took a shower and cleaned up, they could leave. But the first thing was going to be a big breakfast at Hardee's. While Bar Jonah was in the shower, someone knocked on the apartment door, which Roland answered. It was Lori. She told Roland to come back upstairs; there was something she wanted him to hear. When Roland got up to Lori's, she walked over to the telephone answering machine and pushed the button. Messages from seven different men, leaving a message for Bar Jonah, played on the answering machine. Lori was pissed off, saying she wasn't Bar Jonah's fucking secretary and why was he giving out her phone number. He had a phone, why wasn't he using his own number? Lori told Roland to talk with Bar Jonah and tell him not to give out her phone number

18

anymore. She also wanted Roland to tell him that she wasn't his secretary. Roland told Lori she should talk to Bar Jonah, he didn't want to. Sometimes Bar Jonah scared him. Lori told him to stop being a baby and go talk to him like a man.

When Roland went back downstairs, Bar Jonah was standing in the living room in his underwear, towel-drying his hair. Bar Jonah asked Roland where he had been. Roland said upstairs. Bar Jonah told him he wanted to know before he went back up there. Roland sheepishly nodded his head. Then Roland told Bar Jonah about the phone calls and how pissed Lori was. Bar Jonah became enraged. "What do you mean, I had messages and she didn't let me know right away?" Bar Jonah insisted that Roland go back upstairs and tell Lori that he needed to know who had called and what their return phone numbers were. He gave Roland a piece of paper and a chewed-up pencil. Go up and get the names of the men off of the answering machine, Bar Jonah demanded. Get their phone numbers too. I need them for my business. Roland walked back up the stairs with pencil and paper in hand. Bar Jonah knew that he couldn't read or write. How was he supposed to write down their phone numbers? When Roland walked through the door, he told Lori Bar Jonah wanted the names and numbers of the men who had called. Lori told Roland he didn't live there anymore. He couldn't just come barging in on her. Roland began to shake when he heard Lori say that she had already erased the messages.

Roland walked back downstairs. Bar Jonah was sitting on the couch, still in his underwear. He put out his hand telling Roland that he wanted the phone numbers. Roland told him Lori had already got rid of them. Bar Jonah jumped up from the couch and called Lori a fucking bitch, as he walked enraged toward Roland. He reached out and tried to grab Roland by the throat. Roland's neck was fatter than Stanley's. Bar Jonah couldn't get a quick grip on his neck. Roland pulled away and ran toward the front door and ran as fast as he could up the stairs. Bar Jonah was behind him screaming that he was going to kill him. Roland ran into Lori's apartment and tried to hold the door shut. Bar Jonah easily pushed the door open and pinned Roland between the back of the door and the inside wall.

Bar Jonah pushed hard against the door, telling Roland there was no way for him to get away. Roland was sobbing, pleading with Bar Jonah not to hurt him. Bar Jonah slammed the door shut and grabbed Roland around the throat, this time with both hands, making sure he had him tightly in his grip. He started shaking Roland by the neck, screaming that he wouldn't kill him if he'd apologize. Through a mouth of phlegm and mucous, Roland kept saying he was sorry, over and over again. Bar Jonah shoved him into the wall and released his grip from around his neck. Bar Jonah stood staring disgustedly at Roland huddled down in the corner. Roland looked up and tearfully told Bar Jonah he was really hungry and asked if they could still have breakfast together. Bar Jonah looked at Roland and said, "Yeah, I'm going to breakfast, but not with you." Bar Jonah then put a cigarette between his lips, lit it and walked out the door. Roland went through the apartment yelling for Lori. But she had already left for the casino.

Even though he wasn't supposed to, Roland stayed up at Lori's that night. He didn't tell Lori Bar Jonah had choked him. But Roland did tell her that Bar Jonah was mad because he always gave Lori money and he could give out her phone number if he wanted to. She should be bringing him down his phone messages right away. Bar Jonah told Roland his calls were important. There could even be calls for undercover work from the U.S. Marshal's office.

The next morning Roland went back down to Bar Jonah's. Bar Jonah was at the apartment. When he opened the door and saw Roland, he wrapped his arms around him and hugged him close. Roland hugged him back saying how sorry he was for acting up. Bar Jonah pulled Roland into the apartment and told him to sit down, he was going to make him some of his special sausage and eggs for breakfast. Roland saw Bar Jonah take some meat from the refrigerator. It wasn't from a plastic wrapped store-bought package. Roland yelled that he had a stomachache and told Bar Jonah he just wanted eggs for breakfast. Bar Jonah yelled back and said the meat would help his bellyache. "Eat it anyway." Roland sat on the couch and really did become nauseous when he smelled the meat frying. In a few minutes Bar Jonah called for Roland to come and eat. Then he sat down a plate, with sunny-side up eggs and four pieces of hand-pressed greasy sausage patties, in front of Roland and told him to eat up. Roland ate the eggs and picked at the sausage. Bar Jonah stood over him and told him to rub the sausage around in the egg yolks, it was best that way. Roland sopped up as much of the yolk as he could onto the sausage and forced himself to eat it. Bar Jonah massaged Roland's shoulders while he ate to help him relax. It felt so good Roland leaned back against the chair into Bar Jonah's hands. When he was finished, Bar Jonah said they should watch a movie and put *Alive* into the tape player. Roland sat beside Bar Jonah and watched the movie, as he had many times before. Bar Jonah didn't pay much attention to the movie, instead he was writing something in his spiral notebook. Roland looked over a few times, watching Bar Jonah write. It just seemed like a bunch of letters going this way and that in a rectangular grid. Roland couldn't read anyways so it didn't matter much. When the movie was over Bar Jonah said he had to go out and run some errands. He wanted to know if Roland wanted to go with him. Roland said, " Sure." Bar Jonah even promised to buy him a late lunch at Hardee's. Before they left, Bar Jonah told Roland he wanted him to be sure and stay with him that night. He wanted Stormy to stay too. Bar Jonah said he had something fun planned for later.

* * *

Bar Jonah drove over to Bob's and asked him for some money. He said he was short and he needed to buy some food. Bob slipped a few dollars into Bar Jonah's outreached hand. Then Bar Jonah went over to Tyra's and hit her up for some too. She gave him all she had in the house. Tyra said her Social Security check hadn't come in yet, but when it did she would have more to give him. Bar Jonah then stopped at one of the local drug stores and bought a halfdozen disposable cameras. He needed to get some pictures of kids for his toy business, he told Roland. Bar Jonah pulled up in front of Lincoln Elementary School a little before lunch. The kids were getting ants in their pants and squirming in their seats right about now, Bar Jonah quietly said, because they knew the lunch bell was ready to ring anytime. Lunch was always fun for the kids, especially when they got to go outside for playtime before they had to go back to their classrooms. Bar Jonah parked right beside the chain link fence that was mostly there to keep the kids from running out into the street chasing a kick ball. Roland sat in the car while Bar Jonah walked up and down the sidewalk, leaning over the fence, snapping picture after picture of little boys playing. Some of the kids recognized Bar Jonah and came running over to the fence and leaned way too close to the camera for the picture to be in focus, stuck their tongue out and mugged a big grin. Bar Jonah didn't care. He had plenty more pictures that were in focus. It seemed like a big bonus that they liked him taking their picture so much. The little diamond shaped holes in the fence were just the right size for Bar Jonah to slip a Matchbox car or two through to some of the boys that Bar Jonah really liked. He called them his special friends. Bar Jonah liked to give them a toy whenever he had a chance.

When Bar Jonah took all of the pictures on one of the cameras, he would walk back over to the car and pass the used camera through the window to Roland. Then Roland would take a new camera out of its box and give it to Bar Jonah, all ready to go. Bar Jonah wanted Roland to take some pictures too. But Roland said he was way too shy. Bar Jonah said if he was going to be a real photographer he had to get over being shy. Roland told Bar Jonah that he only had one camera left; he had almost used them all up. "Hold onto the last one," Bar Jonah said. He wanted to have one leftover to take some special pictures of Roland and Stormy later on.

Curtain time

As they were driving away from the school, Bar Jonah told Roland that he had to make one more stop before they went home. A few quick rights and lefts and they turned into the post office parking lot. Bar Jonah pulled out a green, certified mail notice. There weren't any other cars in the parking lot. Bar Jonah put his cigarette in the pull-out ashtray and told Roland to leave it alone. He would be back before it would have time to go out. Bar Jonah climbed out of the car and walked into the post office, dangling the green certified mail card from his right hand. The cigarette was still smoldering in the ashtray when Bar Jonah opened the car door and got back in. Roland smiled and told Bar Jonah he hadn't touched the cigarette; he could smell his breath if he wanted to, Roland said. Bar Jonah picked the cigarette up out of the ashtray, slipped it between his lips, drew in a deep lungful of smoke, held it and then slowly let it roll out his nose and over his thin lips. He leaned over close to Roland's face and said, "Blow." Roland, laughing, blew a big breath of air into Bar Jonah's face. Bar Jonah said he didn't smell cigarettes on Roland's breath. He was glad Roland wasn't picking up such a bad habit. Roland laughed and stretched his neck, sniffing the air like a dog looking for stray fumes.

Bar Jonah was carrying a small box. He tossed it to Roland and told him, "Hold it, but don't open it." It was a surprise for later. Roland kept asking Bar Jonah what was in the package all the way back to the apartment. Bar Jonah only repeated not to open it. Usually Bar Jonah would have gotten pissed off at Roland for being so annoying. This time Roland's annoyance brought a smile to his face.

* * *

They got back right when Stormy was bouncing off of the school bus. Bar Jonah grabbed up Stormy and swung him onto his shoulders. Stormy wrapped his hands around Bar Jonah's forehead and leaned back yelling, "Go horsy, go." As they were walking toward Bar Jonah's apartment, Lori drove up. When Lori got out of the car she laughed at Bar Jonah being silly again with Stormy. Bar Jonah told Lori he wanted Stormy to stay overnight with him and Roland. Lori thought it was a good idea because they were having a no limit night on drinks at the casino, so she might be out late anyways. As Lori walked toward the stairs, she yelled for Stormy to have a good time.

* * *

Bar Jonah carried Stormy into his apartment, telling him to duck way down so he didn't bang his head on the doorframe when they went through. Stormy kept trying to put his hands over Bar Jonah's eyes to get him to trip. Bar Jonah kept moving Stormy's hands. Bar Jonah was being so patient with Stormy, even though Stormy was being so trying of Bar Jonah's good-natured patience. Tonight, Bar Jonah was not going to let Stormy's brattiness spoil anything, especially his good mood.

* * *

Roland took a pot from the drying rack and filled it with cold water. Then he put the pot on the stove and turned the burner up to HIGH. He walked over to the refrigerator and took out a brand new package of hot dogs. Bar Jonah said they were going to have a feast. Roland opened the hot dogs and when the water began to boil, he plopped them all into the pot, trying to avoid the splashing hot bubbles when each dog dropped into the water. Bar Jonah came into the kitchen holding the package he had picked up from the post office. Roland excitedly asked Bar Jonah when he was going to tell him what was in the brown box. He wanted to know; it wasn't fair that Bar Jonah was keeping it from him. Bar Jonah ignored his question, simply telling Roland that he was becoming quite the chef, cooking all of the hot dogs by himself. Roland smiled and asked Bar Jonah how many he wanted. Six would be plenty. Roland and Stormy could split the rest. Plus they were also going to have pork and beans with chips. So there'd be plenty to eat. Then after dinner, Bar Jonah was going to show Roland and Stormy what was in the package. Roland laughed and told Bar Jonah he could have an extra hot dog if he showed him now. Bar Jonah told Roland he had bought the hot dogs and he could eat them all if he wanted to.

The pork and beans can opened with a psst when Bar Jonah first squeezed down on the cutting wheel of the can opener. He put another pot on the burner beside the hot dogs. Bar Jonah threw in a half-cup of brown sugar, just for good measure. He untwisted the tie on a pack of hot dog buns, took them out and lined them up side by side, one after another. Then Bar Jonah handed Stormy a big bottle of ketchup and told him to squirt some, but not too much, onto each bun. The water the hot dogs were in was boiling fast and furious now and the dogs were beginning to shrink and split. Bar Jonah glanced into the pot and pronounced them ready to eat. Roland had laid a long strip of paper towels across the kitchen counter and took each hot dog and laid it on the towel to drain. Then he picked up each hot dog with his fingertips, saying ouch every time he dropped one into its waiting bun. Stormy kept running in between Bar Jonah and Roland, yelling that he was hungry. He hadn't eaten lunch at school because Lori had forgotten to give him lunch money. Bar Jonah picked up the plates and placed them on the table. He pulled out a big plastic bottle of soda and said they could all drink it right out of the bottle. There was no reason to dirty a bunch of glasses. Bar Jonah stirred the now hot pork and beans, being sure to mix in the now melted brown sugar. Then he showed the boys how to make a regular hot dog into a gourmet hot dog by spooning on a heaped serving of pork and beans right onto the hot dog itself. He said this was how real chefs ate their hot dogs.

It wasn't long before a round of "mms" from everyoneechoed through the kitchen. Roland quickly ate four and Stormy got the two left over. Bar Jonah finished his six before either Roland or Stormy had finished theirs. The boys started laughing when Bar Jonah leaned back and started rubbing his big, full belly round and round, with the palm of his fat stubby hand. Bar Jonah acted like each time that his hand made a full circle around his belly, it produced a new and bigger belch. Roland and Stormy tried to imitate Bar Jonah but they couldn't burp on command the way Bar Jonah could. Stormy started yelling it wasn't fair that Bar Jonah could burp whenever he wanted. Then Bar Jonah started laughing and lifted one of his butt cheeks. A loud long brrp came from Bar Jonah's ass. "I can fart whenever I want to," Bar Jonah said. Stormy jumped up on his chair, turned around with his butt to the table and started trying to fart. He kept grunting and reaching back, pulling apart his butt cheeks, trying again and again to outdo Bar Jonah. But he couldn't. Roland was laughing so hard he had tears streaming down his face, saying he wanted to try too. Roland stood up from his chair, turned around and promptly ripped a massive fart. A methane-filled fog enveloped the table. Stormy screamed it stunk, jumped off of his chair and ran into the living room, taking rapid, exaggerated breaths along the way. Roland turned around and yelled loudly that he too could fart whenever he wanted. Bar Jonah leaned back in his chair, inhaled deeply and told Roland to do it again.

After Roland farted a few more times, Bar Jonah said it was time to open the package that he and Roland had picked up at the post office. Bar Jonah got up from the table, walked over to the refrigerator and picked the package off of the top, where he had put it just before they sat down to eat. The package was addressed to *Nathan Bar Jonah, U.S. Marshal*. It was from the *National Law Enforcement Supply Company*.

* * *

Bar Jonah proudly announced to Roland if he wanted to become a U.S. Marshal when he got older, that he would put in a good word for him. But usually only men who have done a lot of training on their own can get into the Marshals. They were really choosey about who they gave a badge to because the work was all undercover. Bar Jonah said though that he thought Roland was the kind of person the Marshal service was looking for. With Bar Jonah's recommendation, he was sure Roland could get in if he was sure he wanted to. Roland was now proud too. Stormy started yelling, "Me too, me too." Roland yelled back and told Stormy to shut up. Bar Jonah told Roland he had bought something that would help him get started with his training.

Bar Jonah, as much as possible, liked to have his victims walk with him, hand in hand toward their catastrophic destinies as though they were in a rapturous dream, carried forth by their adoration of Bar Jonah and Bar Jonah alone. He wanted to leave a permanent mark on the boys that he was cultivating to become his successors. In Roland especially, Bar Jonah believed that his legacy would live on. It was almost as good as having a son of his own.

* * *

"You open it," Bar Jonah said. Roland took the package and began to tear the plain brown paper from around the box. When Roland got the paper off, he took the cardboard box and held it out away from him looking at the picture on the front, trying to figure out what it was. Bar Jonah didn't say anything. The picture was of a black, rectangular object with three small curved finger-grooves down each side toward the bottom. At the top were two shiny metal tits. Roland couldn't read the label on the front of the object, so Bar Jonah had to read it to him, "STUN MASTER 100-S". Bar Jonah took the box, opened the flap and pulled apart the form-fitted packaging. There was a small, typed note inside saying the stun gun was charged and ready to use. Bar Jonah took the gun out of the box and commented on its weight. It felt good in his hand. Then Bar Jonah turned off the overhead light. "Watch this," Bar Jonah said to Roland. Stormy was standing beside Bar Jonah, but Bar Jonah was acting like he wasn't there. Bar Jonah held the stun gun in the air and pressed the switch on the left hand side. A slight buzzing sound was emitted from the gun as a blue and orange electrical arc jumped between the two metal tits.

Stormy screamed "Wow" and tried to grab the gun out of Bar Jonah's hand. Bar Jonah pushed him away and told him to mind his own business and to go sit down in the recliner and not to move. Roland asked if he could hold it. Bar Jonah said he was going to do better than that and told Roland to take his shirt off and go lay down on the love seat. Roland got up, pulled his shirt up over his head, walked over and lay down. Bar Jonah, carrying the stun gun, followed behind Roland. Roland lay down on his back, holding his belly on both sides with his hands. He was getting to that age where his belly was beginning to roll away from him if he didn't hold onto it. Bar Jonah joked that big floppy bellies like theirs were the best kind to have because you could put a lot more food in them. Roland laughed every time Bar Jonah made the silly joke.

Bar Jonah stood above Roland, holding the stun gun in his right hand, down at his side, out of sight. Stormy was sitting, rocking the recliner back and forth as hard as he could, smacking the back of the chair into the wall. Bar Jonah didn't seem to notice. Roland watched as Bar Jonah squatted down on his knees beside him. Then Roland only saw the blur as Bar Jonah's

28

right hand came up from his side and shoved the metal tits of the stun gun into one of the fat rolls on Roland's belly.

* * *

For an immeasurable instant, Roland's disquieted eyes met the indifference of Bar Jonah's gaze. Then Bar Jonah pressed the button on the stun gun.

One hundred thousand volts of electricity began surging through Roland's muscles, causing them to feel like they were being microwaved. His arms and legs instantly became rock hard. When the voltage first hit, it caused Roland to take a deep gasp of air far down into his lungs. Then his diaphragm muscle began to immediately lock up, leaving him with a lungful of air that quickly turned into carbon dioxide, making him delirious. Roland's jaw snapped open with such acceleration that his mandible popped loose from his skull. When Bar Jonah smelled that Roland had shit himself, he fixed his pleasured gaze on Roland's stupefied eyes. Then Bar Jonah let up on the button. Roland lay unable to move on the love seat. He was in shock. The havoc that had been wreaked on Roland had lasted but twenty seconds. Stormy ran screaming toward the front door. But Bar Jonah had just a few days before put in a dead bolt that was too high for Stormy to reach. He sat down in front of the door screaming and crying for Bar Jonah to stop hurting Roland. Bar Jonah slipped the stun gun into his pocket, reached up and began slowly stroking Roland's forehead. Roland's muscles were stiff and sore like never before, but he could breathe again. Bar Jonah reached up and gripped Roland's loose-hanging jaw with his left hand and told him to move his mouth up and down. Then when Bar Jonah felt a slack, he slipped Roland's jaw back into place. Roland looked up at Bar Jonah confused. Bar Jonah smiled kindly and told him he had done it before. Roland felt Bar Jonah continue to softly stroke his hair. He leaned in close to Roland's ear and whispered that he had to test him. Bar Jonah put his finger close to his eye and feigned that he was wiping away a tear. Then he told Roland he was proud of him because he had passed the test. He was going to make a great Marshal. Bar Jonah said he was going to let the right people know.

* * *

Fifteen minutes later, Stormy was still sitting against the front door shaking and sniveling, wiping his nose on the cuff of his sleeve. Bar Jonah left Roland lying on the couch, went over and picked up Stormy. Stormy was stiff when Bar Jonah raised him up off of the floor and into his arms. For an instant, Bar Jonah thought Stormy felt like a dead body after a few hours of rigor mortis. Bar Jonah began to rock Stormy and tell him that Roland was okay. Stormy was still whimpering when Bar Jonah pushed his head down onto his shoulder and began rubbing his back. He carried him over to the love seat and squatted down beside Roland, holding Stormy on his knee. Stormy, through a mouthful of mucus, asked Roland if he was all right. Roland nodded that he was. Bar Jonah put Stormy down and told Roland he had to get up. He had laid there long enough, Bar Jonah said, he had to get up off the love seat and clean himself up. Roland complained about how sore his muscles were. Bar Jonah told him the soreness would go away in a few hours. But if he wanted to get into the Marshals, he needed to keep his mouth shut and stop whining. Bar Jonah understood but the other Marshals wouldn't be as kind. They'd see his whining as weak. Bar Jonah stood up and extended his hand down to Roland. When he reached up and took Bar Jonah's hand, Roland felt Bar Jonah jerk him off the love seat. He came up like a board. All of the fluid in his joints felt frozen. He was barely able to make his knees bend enough to fully sit up. He told Bar Jonah that he was still breathing funny. Bar Jonah told Roland not to worry. It would take a few minutes but then he would be able to breathe regular again. He had helped train other Marshals; he knew what stun guns did to people. That was why the Marshals used them.

After a few minutes, Roland said he thought he could get into the bathroom to clean up. Bar Jonah told him to get the love seat cleaned up first; he didn't want it to stink the place up. Roland waddled into the kitchen, pulled the roll of paper towels off the chrome spindle hanging above the sink and carried them back into the living room. He knelt down as best he could and wiped up the area on the couch that he had soiled. Bar Jonah looked and said that was good enough. He should go on and get himself cleaned up. Trying not to make any sounds that would show how much his muscles hurt, Roland used the arm of the love seat to push himself up off of the floor. He noticed he could walk a little less stiffly as he made his way to the bathroom. Roland took off his clothes and rinsed out his underwear in the sink and scrubbed his pants with a washcloth that Bar Jonah had left hanging across the shower rod. When he came back out into the living room, Bar Jonah told him not to sit down on any of the furniture with his pants wet. Roland said he wouldn't. Bar Jonah laughed and told Roland it sounded like he had a mouth full of crap when he talked.

When Roland had gone into the bathroom, Bar Jonah had sat Stormy back down onto the floor and told him to be quiet. He said he didn't want him getting up and running around the apartment, making a lot of noise. Stormy just sat, not making a sound. Roland walked over to Stormy and told him they were going upstairs. He reached down and lifted Stormy up into his arms and walked toward the front door. Roland turned the doorknob and pulled. But the door wouldn't open. Then Roland noticed the dead bolt. He didn't know Bar Jonah had put the dead bolt on the door either. Roland turned the dead-bolt latch, opened the door and started walking up the stairs carrying Stormy. Bar Jonah appeared at the bottom of the stairs and yelled up at Roland. Remember, Bar Jonah said, "Marshal work is top secret. You can't tell anyone or we'll both get into trouble. Do you understand?" Roland yelled back down the stairs that he understood. He wasn't going to say nothing to no one. Roland stayed upstairs that night. The next morning Lori was there. She asked Roland why he wasn't down at Bar Jonah's. Roland said he had moved back upstairs because there wasn't enough room down at Bar Jonah's. Lori nodded and said if that was what Roland wanted, then that was okay with her.

Heartbreak

A few days after Roland moved back upstairs, Bar Jonah called and said he was feeling blue since he had left. They had such fun together. Through Bar Jonah's sniffles, Roland heard him say how much he missed him. Bar Jonah could also hear the tears in Roland's voice when he said that he missed him too. Roland wanted to see Bar Jonah. Could he take him out to eat like they used to? Bar Jonah said he hadn't been feeling real well and was going to try to get to bed early and get some extra rest. Roland's voice sombered when he heard Bar Jonah say no. But he understood. "Maybe another time?" "Yes," Bar Jonah assured Roland. "Another time." This time though, Bar Jonah had just wanted to call and tell Roland how much he was missing him.

* * *

Shortly after he told Roland goodbye, Bar Jonah felt his stomach begin to grumble. He thought he was going to be sick. Before he could get himself up off of the couch, he vomited. That afternoon's lunch just came flying up out of him. He had probably just eaten some spoiled food, he thought. After he cleaned up, Bar Jonah slowly walked down the hallway and fell heavily onto his bed. It was about nine. Somewhere around three a.m., Bar Jonah began rustling out of sleep. As he first began to wake up he thought he had pissed the bed. His sheets were soaked. He was sweating profusely. Then as he pushed himself up, the shooting pains in his left arm began. He tried to stretch out his arm but it was too tight, like he had charley horse in his arm. Each breath came heavier and heavier until he felt like he had a full brick hod sitting on his chest.

The pains continued throughout the night, the morning and into the early afternoon. Right before he got out of bed, about two-thirty in the afternoon, he threw up again. It took everything he had to get over to the hospital. The hospital was across the street from his apartment. Bar Jonah thought it would be just as easy to walk over as to drive. If he collapsed while he was walking, someone would see him go down and call an ambulance. When he presented himself to the triage nurse at the emergency room, he had to lean against the counter to keep from falling over. His face was ashen. His breaths were coming in short, desperate gasps. Later, Bar Jonah said it felt like he was being choked to death. The nurse put him in a nearby wheelchair and pushed him into the treatment area, yelling that she had a possible heart attack.

In seconds, Bar Jonah felt the dollops of electrode paste being put on his chest. Then he watched a nurse attach the heart monitor leads to the silver eyelets of the now secure EKG pads. There was evidence of "persistent ST segment elevation." Bar Jonah was having a myocardial infarction. He was immediately rushed to the Cardiac Cath Lab where an angiogram confirmed that he was suffering from a seventy to eighty percent occlusion of the main arteries of the heart. The artery was opened and stented "in the usual manner with good results." Bar Jonah was then admitted to the Cardiac Intensive Care Unit. The nursing staff there found him just as disagreeable at forty-two as the nurses did when he was ten.

Two days later, Bar Jonah's physician made his rounds and told him that he would need to be in the hospital for another week. Even though the procedure to open up his coronary arteries went well, he was only a couple of days beyond having an infarction. Bar Jonah insisted he couldn't afford it and was leaving against medical advice. His cardiologist tried one last time, explaining that he could die from sudden cardiac death. Bar Jonah wouldn't listen. "You're holding me against my will, just sign my discharge papers," Bar Jonah insisted.

Two months later, Bar Jonah had another myocardial infarction, again at three a.m. When he came into the ER, the same nurse was on duty and he looked the same as he did two months before. The same cardiologist opened the same arteries again. The results were the same, "good." But, again when Bar Jonah insisted on leaving, he was advised that it was risky, especially now that he had had a second heart attack. Just like before Bar Jonah told his doctor that he knew what was best. Before he frustratedly walked out the door, the doctor looked at Bar Jonah and told him that he had better stop smoking. Because of his diabetes and now chronic heart disease, his veins and arteries were in terrible shape. "Especially," he said, "with that leg of yours. If you don't take care of that thing, it's going to end up killing you." He went on to chastise Bar Jonah's smoking and obesity. It was making a bad problem worse and putting his life even more at risk. Bar Jonah nodded and thanked him this time and said he wanted to quit too. The doctor took the time to tell Bar Jonah about a smoking cessation program that the hospital ran. They could help. That was why they were there. He knew that smoking was a tough taskmaster. Every day he had to deal with patients who were gravely ill or who had died because they couldn't stop smoking. Bar Jonah said he would be sure and pray for his doctor's other patients.

As he was waiting for the traffic to slow so he could cross the street in front of the hospital, Bar Jonah noticed that his right leg was stiff. When he was sedentary for very long, it was as though his scar would be begin to draw up on him. Then when he'd stretch his leg back out, it would feel like old, dry deer hide. That always made him nervous. He lighted up a cigarette to help calm him down.

Passover

July 4th was a big day for Roland. Back on the reservation, fireworks were everywhere. A lot of the Indians spent a whole month's allotment check on fireworks when the fourth rolled around. Hong Kong Harry dropped converted railroad cars, turned into makeshift fireworks stands, wherever there was an empty field with an electrical hookup. Things were different down in Great Falls though. There were only certain fireworks you could set off in the city and Roland didn't think much of sparklers and bottle rockets. He liked to celebrate *his* birthday with a bang, the bigger, the better. About ten p.m. on July 3rd, Bar Jonah told Roland he had a surprise for him. "Go sit down on the couch," Bar Jonah said to Roland. "You're going to get your birthday present a day early."

Bar Jonah walked down the hallway and into his bedroom. In no time he came lumbering back down the hallway, bouncing for effect off one wall into the other, grunting and acting like he could barely carry the big box he had wrapped in special, shiny paper. Roland was so excited. He had never even seen a birthday box so big. The big kidder Bar Jonah yelled that Roland was going to snap his head off his shoulders if he didn't stop twisting his neck so far around, trying to see what Bar Jonah was carrying. "Come on and hurry up," Roland would say, over and over again. Finally Bar Jonah made it into the living room with what looked like the heaviest box ever. Bar Jonah had to bend his knees so he could set the box down onto the floor without dropping it. Then Bar Jonah told Roland to watch as he reached up and took the shade off a lamp sitting on an end table. Bar Jonah grabbed the box between his hands and tipped it up onto one of its corners. Then he slowly began to rotate the box in the light of the bare bulb. The hundreds of candles that were imprinted on the mirrored wrapping paper looked like they were flickering wildly under the light. Roland exclaimed a loud "Wow!" Bar Jonah told Roland to make a wish and blow out the candles. Roland took a deep breath and blew a stream of warm air out of his mouth with a resounding whoosh, right as Bar Jonah flicked off the switch on the light, making the room momentarily dark. Bar Jonah reached over and picked up the nicotine-stained accordion shade and slipped the hole atop the brass wire frame back over the threads, protruding from the top of the lamp. He snatched up the wing nut he had laid on the end table and with a quick spin, tightened the shade over the light once more. Then Bar Jonah's short, yellowed fingers pushed the brown plastic switch from off to on, making the room bright again.

* * *

Roland was trembling with excitement. Usually everyone at his house just got excited about our country's birthday, Roland said. He sure didn't ever remember anyone doing something so nice for him like Bar Jonah had just done. And he hadn't even unwrapped his birthday present yet. Bar Jonah said Roland should go ahead and open up the box. Roland reached down and gripped the edges of the box real tight because he thought the box was so heavy that he was going to need a burst of strength to lift it. Roland steadied himself and jerked the box upward. The box came flying off of the floor like it had been launched, causing Roland to lose his balance and fall onto Bar Jonah's ever present belly. Roland started laughing hysterically, saying "You kidded me, I thought it was heavy. You kidded me, you're the big kidder." Bar Jonah tickled Roland and told him if he didn't open the box he was going to take it away. "Kidder," Roland said again.

Roland's hands were a haze of motion as he tore the paper from the big tan cardboard box. When he pulled enough of the paper off to peel open the top flaps and peer down into the box, Roland could barely believe what he saw. Inside were six boxes of M-80s and aerial repeaters. Roland knew just what they were. Picking up one of the repeaters, Roland told Bar Jonah they were called "cakes" on the reservation because they made so many people happy when they blew up. Roland stayed up past midnight, picking up the thin cartons with the M-80s stacked on top on each other like tiny depth charges, turning them around in his hands, staring for the longest time at the exploding red and yellow starbursts printed on the side of each box. Before Bar Jonah went to bed, he told Roland that he would take him out to the old caves, further out on 26th Street, when it got dark on the 4th. It was out of the city limits so they wouldn't have to worry about being bothered by the cops.

Roland went ahead and slept on Bar Jonah's couch that night, waking up to the smoke of Bar Jonah's first cigarette of the day wafting through the apartment. Bar Jonah walked over to Roland, called him a sleepyhead and handed him a cup of strong coffee with real cream and lots of sugar. Bar Jonah asked Roland if he wanted Stormy and Stanley to go with them when they set off the fireworks. Roland said *no*. He wanted it to be a special time just with him and Bar Jonah. Bar Jonah said okay and that he had to go to work. He told Roland to lock up when he left and that he would be back about five. Roland should be ready to go when he got back. Bar Jonah was going to take him out for a big birthday dinner too.

* * *

Roland was looking out the window when he saw Bar Jonah's old station wagon pull into the parking lot. The big birthday box of fireworks was sitting right beside Roland's right leg waiting to be picked up and taken out to the caves, where they would be ignited and brought to life. This time Roland was ready for the lightness of the box and didn't lose his balance when he picked it up.

Roland sat the box down by the front door, turned the doorknob and pulled the door open. He pushed the box out onto the landing with his foot, reached around with his hand and started to pull the door shut behind him. When Roland pulled on the doorknob he felt a resistance. He looked up and saw Lori pushing her round flat face through the crack between the door and frame. "Don't smush my face," Lori said. "I just wanted to tell you happy birthday and have fun tonight." Roland eagerly nodded his head up and down and said he would. He picked up the box and started walking down the stairs. When he was almost at the bottom of the stairs, Roland heard Lori yell to be sure and say hi to Bar Jonah.

* * *

Bar Jonah was just about to put the key into the door lock, when he saw the storm door at the entrance to the stairs fly open and start to bounce back hard against its worn spring. Roland's foot was at the ready, stopping the door from smacking into him. The big birthday box, held by two brown hands, came pushing out of the door first. Roland was so excited when he saw the top of Bar Jonah's head that he stumbled and fell. The door got away from his boot and smacked him in the nose, making it start to bleed. Bar Jonah leaned down and told Roland he was okay, it was just a little blood. Nothing that he couldn't live without. Roland's bright eyes and big smile gave away how proud he was of himself that he hadn't dropped the box or cried. Bar Jonah extended his hand and helped Roland stand up. "Are you hungry?" Bar Jonah asked, as Roland got to his feet. Roland said he sure was. Bar Jonah told Roland to go ahead and put the box into his car. He wanted to get something for Roland to look at while they drove to the all-you-can-eat place for dinner. Roland worked the box into the back seat of Bar Jonah's car and climbed into the front seat, slipping the shoulder strap across his broad chest. A few minutes later, Bar Jonah came out of his apartment carrying a couple of fat, black, three-ring binders. He walked around to Roland's side of the car and passed the binders to him through the open window, telling Roland not to drop them. As Bar Jonah backed his car out of the parking lot, he told Roland to open up the binders and take a look at the pictures. When Roland flipped the top binder open he saw pictures of kids. Thousands of pictures of young boys, page after page, that Bar Jonah had put into plastic baseball card sleeves. Bar Jonah told Roland he had taken most of them himself. Some of them he had just cut out of magazines though. Roland thumbed through each plastic sleeve and told Bar Jonah that he sure was a good photographer. Bar Jonah reminded Roland that he was a good photographer too.

* * *

It took just a few quick turns to get to *Evelyn's All You Can Eat* further out on 10th. Bar Jonah jumped out of the car first and said he was going to race Roland to the door. Roland put the binders on the floor, jumped out of the car and followed Bar Jonah, yelling that it wasn't fair that Bar Jonah got a giant head start.

When the hostess came to seat Bar Jonah and Roland, Bar Jonah gave her his name and told her that he and his boy were hungry. They wanted a big table, where they could spread out lots of food. Bar Jonah and Roland followed the hostess, zigzagging through the labyrinth of other eaters. When they got to their table, there was a rectangular piece of laminated cardboard, folded in half with the word "RESERVED", in bold black letters, printed on both sides. Bar Jonah had called ahead; he wanted this to be Roland's special day.

* * *

The buffet was filled with just about everything anyone could want, roast beef, ham and prime rib, something Roland had never heard of before. Bar Jonah told Roland that when he was a chef he used to wear a toque, just like the chef who was carving the prime rib. Roland told Bar Jonah he thought he'd like to be a chef instead of a U.S. Marshal.

Bar Jonah and Roland lost count of the number of times they went back through the buffet. But Roland said he didn't think he'd ever be able to eat again. Bar Jonah laughed and said they hadn't even had dessert yet. Roland said it didn't matter. About that time, Roland looked up from his plate and saw a procession of troubadours, disguised as waitresses and waiters converging on their table. At the same time, Roland's ear caught wind of the troupe singing, "Happy birthday to you, happy birthday to you, happy birthday dear Roland, happy birthday to you."

The waiter leading the pageantry was carrying a chocolate chip cupcake with a sparkler sending off silver blue sparks in every direction. When the waiter sat the cupcake down in front of Roland, the parade of singers began loudly clapping and then turned around and walked away.

With tears streaming down his face, Roland took a deep, excited breath that unfolded his chest and made him feel buoyant in his chair. He tried so hard to blow out the sparkler that it seemed like his head should be going backward instead of forward. Roland blew over and over again, until he had no breath left. He looked up pleadingly at Bar Jonah. There was a slight psst, after Bar Jonah dipped his fingers in his water glass, reached across the table and snuffed out the flame between his thumb and forefinger.

Roland pulled the thin metal dowel out of the cupcake and laid it on a napkin beside the plate. He pulled away the cupcake wrapper and asked Bar Jonah if he wanted a bite. Bar Jonah said no, it was just for him. Roland picked up the cupcake and said that even though he was the fullest he'd *ever* been, he was still going to eat the whole thing. Bar Jonah applauded when Roland pushed the last bite into his mouth and then licked the icing off of his fingertips. After that, they sat for a few minutes and Bar Jonah said he thought it was dark enough for them to go and shoot off the fireworks. As they were walking out of the restaurant, Roland leaned against Bar Jonah, clutching the remains of the burned out sparkler in his right hand, saying it was for sure the best birthday he'd ever had.

* * *

They drove back down 10th Avenue until they got to 26th Street. Bar Jonah swung his old station wagon around the corner as he flipped the burned out end of his cigarette out the window and headed west. An ambulance, with its red lights flashing and siren wailing started to turn in front of Bar Jonah into the ER entrance of the hospital, just off to the left. Bar Jonah swerved and cut in front of the ambulance, causing the ambulance driver to slam on its brakes. Roland chided Bar Jonah and said that you were always supposed to stop for ambulances. Bar Jonah said he was there first. It didn't take long until the paved road turned to gravel. Roland was getting more and more excited; the caves were just a short ways away.

* * *

The sun had just tucked itself in for the night when Bar Jonah and Roland got up to the caves. Bar Jonah turned off of the gravel road and drove up over a couple of dirt mounds, causing the car to teeter for a second like a plate on a stick. Roland felt the hard tip of the dirt mounds scraping the bottom of the car. Bar Jonah made Roland giggle when he called the dirt mounds land titties. After bouncing over a couple of titties, Bar Jonah brought the car to a stop. Roland swung his legs out of the car door, got his birthday box from the back seat and carried it over to a small clearing. Bar Jonah walked behind Roland carrying a couple of empty five-gallon metal cans that he had taken from Hardee's. The cans had been filled with floor wax, but Bar Jonah had poured the wax down the drain one night after he had closed up the restaurant.

41

Roland took out all the boxes of M-80's and spread them out on the ground. Bar Jonah picked up one of the wax cans and walked out about fifty yards, waving his hand in the air for Roland to follow. Roland grabbed a handful of M-80's and shoved them into his pockets, as he took off running toward Bar Jonah. Bar Jonah stopped and squatted down next to a large flat rock, laying the can down on its side. "Come down here," Bar Jonah said to Roland. When Roland squatted down and sat back on his heels, he asked Bar Jonah what he was going to do. Bar Jonah reached out and handed Roland an old silver flip-top lighter. Then Bar Jonah told Roland he wanted him to lay one of the M-80's on the rock, light the fuse, put the metal can upside down over the M-80 and then run as fast as he could back to the car. "Think you can do it without getting blown up?" Bar Jonah asked Roland. Roland nodded his head up and down. Bar Jonah said he would go on back to the car and give Roland the signal when to light the fuse. Bar Jonah stretched up slowly and walked back to the car. When he got back, Bar Jonah took cover behind the driver's side fender and yelled for Roland to light the fuse.

Roland flipped open the lighter and rolled the flint wheel several times, before it lighted. Then he leaned his head back, and inhaled deeply when the benzene aroma of lighter fluid reached his nostrils. The fuse felt hard as Roland twisted the tip between his fingers, to make it easier to light. Then Roland cupped his hand around the fuse and touched the yellow flame to the gray cordite-infused wick. A hissing pink, crimson and scarlet glow began to scream its way down the fuse. Roland nervously reached out to pick up the metal can when he lost his balance and fell back off his heels. Bar Jonah screamed for Roland to hurry up. Roland scrambled around, grabbed the can, sat it over the M-80, quickly stood up and took off running toward Bar Jonah's car. Bar Jonah yelled that Roland had better move his butt, or he was going to get blown up. Out of breath, Roland ran around to the side of the car and slammed into Bar

Jonah. Bar Jonah and Roland quickly jerked their heads around right before the M-80 exploded, shooting the wax can twenty feet into the air. Roland jumped to his feet, screaming, "Did you see that, did you see that?!" Bar Jonah patted Roland on the shoulder and said, "Happy birthday." Roland, grinning from ear to ear, turned to Bar Jonah and told him again it was the best birthday that he'd ever had. Bar Jonah told Roland to go and blow the can up again. But this time he couldn't be so clumsy or he might get his fingers blown off. "You have to put the can where you can get right to it without thinking," Bar Jonah patiently explained. "That way you have everything planned out and you won't get yourself in trouble." Roland, barely able to stand still, nodded his head that he understood and then tore off running back toward the flat rock, yelling that this time he was going to blow the can all the way up to the moon.

Roland walked over and picked up the wax can and carried it back to the flat rock. Then he squatted down and took an M-80 out of his pocket. He laid it on the center of the rock and stretched the fuse out a bit and twisted up the end. Then he took a small rock and sat it a few inches from the M-80. When Roland sat the can over the M-80 he carefully positioned the lip of the can on top of the rock, allowing the fuse to stick out from underneath the can a couple of inches. Roland felt a sense of pride when he looked back and saw Bar Jonah nodding his head up and down. The lighter's wick was still wet with fluid when Roland flicked the knurled flint wheel. The flame uncurled out of the lighter like a snake's tongue, as Roland laid the fire to the sharp tip of the fuse. The fuse fired and took off. But this time so did Roland. Bar Jonah was standing behind the car egging him on. "Come on, come on, hurry up, you can make it," Bar Jonah yelled.

Roland was running so fast that he couldn't stop and went flying over the hood of the car. Bar Jonah caught Roland as he was sliding off the hood, just in time to whirl him around, so he could hear the report of the M-80 and see the can disappear into the sky. Bar Jonah smiled when he told Roland that he thought he saw the wax can bounce off of the moon. Roland flipped over on his back, pulled his legs up to his chest and started spinning in circles on top of the hood of the car. Bar Jonah said if he didn't stop he was going to make himself throw up.

* * *

Standing up inside Roland's birthday box were a dozen tubes about eighteen inches long, with two-inch openings at the top end. The tubes were glued to an octagonal piece of heavy cardboard. Thick Chinese characters and angry red dragons stenciled on the side of the tubes said to Roland that these were extra special cakes. Roland left the rest of the M-80s by the car and carried the cakes out to the flat rock. Bar Jonah said he would follow Roland this time. Roland lifted one of the cakes out of the box and looked down the tube at the red tissue paper wadding. Then he sat the tube on the rock and pulled out the fuse. Bar Jonah walked back about ten feet and sat down on the ground, folding his legs underneath him. When Roland looked back, he saw Bar Jonah lighting a cigarette. Roland ran over to Bar Jonah and asked him if he was ready. Bar Jonah looked up and said through his smoke tinged voice that he couldn't wait. Roland ran back and squatted down beside the cake. He took the lighter out of his pants pocket, and like an expert, flipped open the pot metal lid with his thumb and lit the fuse. Roland pushed himself up with his knees, dashed back and sat down close to Bar Jonah, leaning into his shoulder.

Bar Jonah's and Roland's heads cocked at the very moment the cake shot its glowing orange fireball whistling three hundred feet into the air. A few seconds later, the cake exploded, sending an array of colorful chrysanthemum fire flowers bursting open against the night sky. Bar Jonah and Roland pushed against each other's shoulders and uttered, in what seemed to be one voice, a loud "Ooh!" Roland told Bar Jonah that he wanted him to shoot off one too. Bar Jonah was the one who had made his birthday so special, he should have fun too. Roland, feeling embarrassed, hung his head slightly when Bar Jonah said no, it was Roland's special night. But Bar Jonah thanked him for being so courteous.

* * *

A sheriff's deputy was driving by when he saw the cakes flaring in the sky. He pulled off the road, got out of his cruiser, walked up to Bar Jonah and Roland and said hello. Bar Jonah and Roland extended their hands in friendship to the sheriff. He offered his back in kind. The officer said he just wanted to make sure it wasn't a bunch of underage kids, shooting off fireworks without adult supervision. Some kid had lost a finger or two earlier in the evening by not having an adult there to keep an eye on things. Some parents will let their kids do anything, the officer said. Bar Jonah told the sheriff that he would never let his son, even though he was older, play around with fireworks without him being there. The sheriff nodded in agreement. Roland invited the officer to stay while he shot off the last cake. The officer told him he would if Roland could make it fast. He had to get back out on patrol. Roland ran out to the rock, set up the cake, lit the fuse and ran back to where Bar Jonah and the sheriff were standing. A few seconds later, the final aerial tribute of the night to the birth of the United States and Roland Big Leggins adorned the night sky.

Before the sheriff left, Bar Jonah told Roland to clean everything up. He didn't want to leave the place a mess. The officer thanked Bar Jonah and Roland for the show, reached out and shook their hands and made his way back to his car. A few minutes later, after the sheriff had pulled away, Roland was still searching for debris from the fireworks. Bar Jonah told him not to bother, they had to go. Roland said he couldn't wait to get home because he was hungry again. Bar Jonah suggested that they run over to Hardee's. It was open late and they could pick up some sandwiches and then call it a night. Roland thought that was a real good idea. Before they left, Bar Jonah picked up the now deformed wax cans and gave them a big toss toward one of the caves, far away from the flat rock. Roland asked Bar Jonah why he didn't want to take them back home and throw them away. Bar Jonah said it was best to leave them, maybe someone else could use them for something. He didn't like things to go to waste. Roland said that seemed like a good idea. They got back into the car, bounced their way over the land titties and pulled back out onto the gravel road. Hardee's was just up the road so it didn't take long to get there. When they went into the restaurant, Bar Jonah walked behind the counter and loaded up a couple of bags with doublecheese burgers and fries. Roland knew that Bar Jonah ran the place, so it was okay when he strolled out from behind the counter, carrying the bags of food without paying for them. Bar Jonah looked at Roland and said they could just eat in the car on the way home. Roland took the burgers Bar Jonah handed him, as they squeezed side-by-side through the glass doors. As he was dropping his car into reverse, Bar Jonah looked out the wind-shield and saw the shift manager standing behind the counter giving him the finger. Bar Jonah smiled, backed his car out of the parking spot in front of the restaurant, pulled the gear shift on the steering column down to drive and drove away. Before Bar Jonah had pulled back out onto 10th, he had already eaten one of his six burgers. Roland was pushing a wad of fries into his mouth, muttering something to Bar Jonah how good they were when they were real hot and salty. Bar Jonah told Roland that it was impolite to talk with his mouth full.

* * *

Lori was pulling into the parking lot right at the same time that Bar Jonah and Roland were getting back. Roland jumped out of the car when he saw Lori. He ran up to Lori and started tell-ing her how much fun he and Bar Jonah had had. Stanley and

46

Stormy got out of the car complaining they hadn't gotten to go with Bar Jonah and Roland. Roland told Stanley to keep his mouth shut, it wasn't his birthday. Stormy wouldn't be quiet either, so Roland thumped him on the head with his knuckles and told him to go upstairs to bed. "It was too late for a kid to be up anyway," Roland said. Lori walked over to Bar Jonah, put her arms around his neck and kissed him, saying how nice it was of him to make Roland's birthday so special. Bar Jonah said it was special for him too. Roland was like a son to him.

CHAPTER THREE

Roland and Stanley

On the morning of July 5th, Bar Jonah left early and was gone until late in the afternoon. Roland and Stanley had been watching for him. When they heard his car pull into the driveway about three, Roland and Stanley went running out of Lori's front door. Roland grabbed the banisters on each side of the stairway, lifted himself in the air and swung his feet forward, taking three steps at a time. Stanley started swinging down the banisters too, but he didn't wait until Roland was enough out of the way and kicked him in the back of the head. Roland didn't seem to mind though and just kept doing what Bar Jonah had once called his flying three-step. Bar Jonah had heard them jumping down the stairs, before they got to the landing. He kidded them and said it sounded like they were wearing clodhoppers because they were making so much noise. Bar Jonah said he was glad they had come down, because he was going to come up and get them if they hadn't.

* * *

Barry hadn't been around much in recent weeks, but it so happened that when Bar Jonah, Roland and Stanley went into the apartment, they found Barry sitting on the couch. Bar Jonah turned around and locked the door once they were all inside. Stanley noticed right away that the sheet Bar Jonah had covering the kitchen was gone. Bar Jonah told Stanley to go and sit with Barry on the couch and watch television. He wanted to talk to Roland privately. Stanley went over and flipped on the black and white television, adjusted the rabbit ears and sat down beside Barry. Barry nodded at Stanley. Bar Jonah walked over, handed Stanley a new bag of potato chips and then told Roland to come back to his bedroom. Roland giddily followed Bar Jonah down the hallway. When Bar Jonah and Roland walked through the door, Bar Jonah turned around, slammed the door and pushed the lock button on the tarnished brass-plated knob.

Roland was standing by the bed grinning when Bar Jonah turned around and ordered him to pull his pants down. Roland's face turned sour and said "No," he wasn't going to do it and started to walk toward the bedroom door. Bar Jonah, with a searing glare, pushed his chest out, stepped in front of Roland and blocked his way. He reached over and roughly unbuckled Roland's belt and yanked the jeans down over Roland's protruding belly. Roland grabbed the waist of his pants, trying to stop Bar Jonah from pulling them farther down. Bar Jonah easily jerked Roland's pants out of his hands, pulling them all the way down to his ankles. Then he reached up and before Roland could stop him, dropped Roland's boxers. Roland stood exposed and frozen. "Why was Bar Jonah doing this to me," Roland kept asking himself. Bar Jonah stuck his hand out and grabbed Roland's penis. Roland involuntarily started getting hard as Bar Jonah crudely started yanking on his penis. When Bar Jonah let Roland's penis go so he could pull down his own sweat pants, Roland's penis embarrassingly flipped up and smacked the bottom of his belly. After Bar Jonah pushed down his sweat pants, he took his left hand and lifted his belly, so he could reach his penis with his right hand. Bar Jonah squeezed his penis between his thumb and forefinger and began stroking, trying unsuccessfully to get hard. Bar Jonah was getting pissed. He told Roland to get him hard. Roland said he didn't want to touch Bar Jonah's wiener. Bar Jonah reached out with his right hand, took Roland's wrist and pulled his hand towards his penis. "Touch me," Bar Jonah ordered. Bar Jonah was still lifting his belly when he felt Roland's fingers curl around his penis. Roland stood holding Bar Jonah's penis, while Bar Jonah now held up his belly with both hands. Other than trembling, Roland's hand remained motionless on Bar Jonah's penis.

Stanley and Barry were still sitting in the living room. They both had a sense something was wrong. It wasn't that there were any loud sounds coming from Bar Jonah's bedroom, it was more that there weren't any.

* * *

Suddenly, someone started pounding on Bar Jonah's bedroom door. It was Stanley, screaming, wanting to know if Roland was okay. Barry also hollered back, wanting to know if something was wrong. Bar Jonah screamed for Stanley to get the fuck away from the door. He ignored Barry. Stanley continued to scream and kick the door. Barry stayed sitting on the couch. When Stanley started kicking the door, Roland let go of Bar Jonah's dick, stepped back and bumped the back of his legs into the bed rails. When Roland knew he had enough room, he quickly reached down and pulled up his boxers and jeans. Bar Jonah was now screaming at Stanley, to get the away from the door, before he came out of the bedroom and killed him. Once Roland had buckled his jeans, he sat down on the bed, not speaking. Bar Jonah moved his hands, letting his belly drop, reached down and pulled up his sweat pants. Then Bar Jonah jerked the door open, just as Stanley was drawing back his foot to kick the door again. "What the fuck are you doing," Bar Jonah screamed at Stanley. Stanley was stretching

51

his neck, yelling at Roland, asking him if he was okay. Roland, in a shame-soaked voice, said that he was. Roland stood up from the bed and started to push past Bar Jonah. Bar Jonah put his arm over the door; Roland meekly stopped. The callous, spiteful eyes of Bar Jonah captured Roland's confused and shocked eyes. "You are never to tell *anyone* about this. Do you understand?" Bar Jonah demanded. He was pleased when he heard Roland's humiliated voice tearfully say that he would never say "nothin' to nobody." Bar Jonah lowered his arm and let Roland squeeze past. Stanley was now pinned between the bedroom door and the end of the hallway.

Roland took off running toward the front door. Halfway down the hallway Roland broke down and started sobbing. He felt like he was going to vomit. Bar Jonah effortlessly pushed his forearm against Stanley's mouth when he began to yell for Roland not to leave him. Echoing against the panic inside his head, Roland could barely make out an unintelligible voice that may have been Stanley's. But no matter what, Roland couldn't stop his legs from making him run away.

Roland ran out of Bar Jonah's apartment, turned left and started to walk toward the caves, where he and Bar Jonah had celebrated his happy birthday just the day before. Reaching them an hour later, he sat down on the flat rock and wiped his wet eyes with his shirtsleeve. Roland fingered the remains of the fireworks still lying around, until long after the sun had gone to sleep.

* * *

As soon as Roland slammed the front door behind him, Bar Jonah grabbed Stanley's shoulder and began violently shaking him, angrily saying that he had something to show Stanley in the kitchen. Bar Jonah dragged Stanley down the hallway, telling him he was going to like his surprise. Barry saw Bar Jonah take Stanley over to the kitchen table, push him down on a chair and tell him not to move. Bar Jonah walked over to a paint-splattered wooden buffet and opened the second drawer. He pulled out a dark yellow-stained rope, with a noose tied at one end. When Barry saw Bar Jonah pull the rope out of the drawer, he jumped up and asked Bar Jonah what he was going to do with the rope. Bar Jonah told him that it was none of his fucking business. Barry said he didn't want anything to do with what Bar Jonah was up to. He turned and walked down the hallway to his room, where Barry closed and locked his door. Stanley yelled from the kitchen, asking what Bar Jonah was going to do with the rope. Bar Jonah looked at Stanley and said that the rope was his surprise. Stanley jumped off of the chair and made a run for the door. But before he even got close, he was scooped up in the crook of Bar Jonah's arm. Bar Jonah carried Stanley under his left arm, kicking and screaming, back into the dining room. He stepped up onto a wooden chair, still holding Stanley under his arm, reached up and fed the end of the rope over the rubber pulley, hanging from the ceiling joist. When Bar Jonah stepped back down off of the chair, he pulled the rope with him, making the noose just the right height for Stanley. Bar Jonah kicked the chair out of the way with his foot and flipped Stanley back up onto his feet, while quickly slipping the rope over Stanley's neck. Then he pulled on the other end of the rope, tightening the noose. When Stanley felt the noose gripping his throat, he was sure he was going to die. The rough hemp of the rope cut into Stanley's Adam's apple and the back of his jaw. He tried to tell Bar Jonah that he couldn't breathe but he didn't have enough air to push the words out of his mouth. Stanley was standing on his tip-toes, trying to give himself more air. Each time Stanley pushed himself up with his toes, Bar Jonah smiled, leaned close to Stanley's face, stared contemptuously and unsympathetically into his eyes and pulled the noose tighter. Stanley could just barely get enough height to continue to be able to breathe. When Bar Jonah had Stanley just where he wanted him, he tied the other end of the rope to the handle on the oven. Bar Jonah got down on his knees and unbuckled Stanley's pants and in one swift yank pulled down Stanley's jeans and underwear. Stanley tried to kick Bar Jonah with one foot but he lost his balance, only to be caught by the noose.

He was hanging now, strangling, thrashing around, panicking. Stanley couldn't figure out how to get his legs back underneath him. Bar Jonah let Stanley think that he *was* going to die, then he wrapped his left arm around Stanley's waist, stroked his hair with his right hand and gently lifted him, letting him capture a quick breath and again feel his toes against the floor. "Stand still," Bar Jonah whispered softly, leaning in close to Stanley's ear, letting him know that he understood his predicament. Then Bar Jonah reached out and began to fondle Stanley's penis. It became hard in Bar Jonah's hand. Bar Jonah softly whispered again in Stanley's ear how much he must like it, otherwise he wouldn't have gotten hard. Stanley uselessly kept trying to scream, as Bar Jonah reached around and kept squeezing his butt. Stanley was now too paralyzed with fear to try to pull away. He knew that if he lost his balance again, and Bar Jonah didn't save him, he would strangle to death. Bar Jonah murmured how much he liked how sweaty Stanley smelled.

* * *

Barry yelled from his bedroom that he had to leave for work in a few minutes. Bar Jonah yelled back and told him to stay put. Barry yelled louder that he couldn't. He had to be on time or else he'd be fired. Barry said he was coming out. Bar Jonah pulled Stanley's underwear and pants back up. He left his buckle dangling open. Bar Jonah stood up and untied the end of the rope from the oven door, keeping the tension on the rope with his hand. He grabbed Stanley by the jaw and told him that he was to keep his mouth shut. Stanley's voice was gravelly like a smoker's, when he promised that he would. Bar Jonah lowered the rope and slipped the noose back over Stanley's head. Stanley reached up and rubbed his hands around his rope-burned neck. Bar Jonah roughly pushed Stanley's head back, pulled his hands away from his neck and said that it looked okay. He'd be fine. Stanley's legs were wobbly and his breathing was quick and shallow. Bar Jonah lifted Stanley up by the shoulders and sat him on a kitchen chair. He told him to stay put while he got a warm, wet washcloth to clean him up. Stanley sat like he was cast in iron, staring into nowhere. Bar Jonah came back, bent down and looked at Stanley's face. Stanley's nose and lips were caked with dried snot. His dark, brown skin looked tattooed with the stains of salty tears. Bar Jonah smirked and told Stanley that his face had turned into a pinto bean.

* * *

Bar Jonah cleaned Stanley up and told him to go home. Before he walked out the door, Bar Jonah reminded Stanley that he must have liked it a lot because he sure got hard. He'd better keep his mouth shut, Bar Jonah said, or everyone would know. Stanley also heard Bar Jonah say that they weren't any different, as he pulled the door close. Bar Jonah yelled to Barry that he could come out now and go on to work. Barry timidly came walking down the hallway and saw the noose lying on the kitchen table. He said there wasn't any sense in going to work because he was already late; he had probably been fired anyways.

"Lord, how many times shall I forgive my brother?"

Roland and Stanley didn't go back down to Bar Jonah's for about a week. Bar Jonah happened to see them getting off the school bus and walked up to them, just to see how they were doing. He also thought it would be fun to go to a movie. There was something special playing at the cinema. Bar Jonah wanted to take Roland and Stanley to see it. He wasn't going to tell them what the movie was though, it was going to be a surprise. They could bring Stormy too. Stanley said, no thanks, he didn't want to go. Roland asked Bar Jonah when they could go. Bar Jonah said that night would be good for him because he didn't have to work. Roland told Stanley he really should go too. It would be fun. Stanley stood shaking his head, no. Bar Jonah said he would pick up Roland and Stormy about six-thirty. They could grab something to eat after the movie. Roland liked that idea.

At six-thirty, Bar Jonah was knocking on Lori's door, yelling that they needed to get going so they could get a good seat. Bar Jonah was startled when Lori jerked open the door and sarcastically asked Bar Jonah what he wanted. He said he was picking up Roland and Stormy to take them to the movies. Lori apologized, saying she and Gerald had been fighting and she didn't mean to take it out on him. Bar Jonah reached through the door and hugged Lori saying that he understood. Lori knew she could always get a sympathetic shoulder from Bar Jonah. He always understood.

Roland came bounding out of his bedroom yelling that he was ready. Stormy ran out the door and hugged Bar Jonah's leg. Stanley was sitting inert on the couch. Lori looked at Bar Jonah and said she couldn't get Stanley to do nothin'. "He just wants to sit around all day," Lori said. Lori complained that Stanley used to be a real good helper, but the past week or so he hadn't wanted to do anything. Bar Jonah leaned his head through the door and told Stanley he had enough money to take him to the movies too, if he wanted to go. Roland came out about that time and told Stanley he should go, that it would be fun. Stanley got up and lethargically walked toward the door. He looked at Bar Jonah and snottily told him to move out of the way so he could get by. Bar Jonah caught Lori's eyes and shook his head in sympathy of her plight. Roland walked up to Lori, hugged her and told her she was a good mom and not to wait up for him. They'd probably be out late. Lori said she was going out later too, so she may not even be home when the boys got back. Stanley didn't say a word on the drive to the cinema. Roland and Stormy didn't shut up.

* * *

When they all got their tickets, Stanley walked away from Bar Jonah, Roland and Stormy, and went into the theatre by himself. Stanley looked around the dimly lit theatre and found a spot where there was only one seat available. He walked over and sat down beside an older man, who was also sitting alone and who had not yet taken off his cowboy hat. Stanley ignored Bar Jonah, Roland and Stormy when they walked by. The man sitting beside Stanley tried to strike up a conversation with him, but Stanley ignored him too. After the movie started, Stanley heard Bar Jonah, Roland and Stormy laughing. Stanley could also hear Stormy making fart sounds.

When the movie was over, Stanley jumped up and ran out to the lobby ahead of Bar Jonah, Roland and Stormy. Stanley was leaning against a coming attraction's poster when he saw them all walk out of the theater together. Bar Jonah was laughing and shoving Roland into other customers, as they made their way out to the lobby. Right as they walked in front of the candy counter, Bar Jonah pushed Roland hard into a woman, who was with a man whose arms were inked with black cobras, slithering through the eyes of a red skull. The woman's popcorn went flying into the air, like it was having a second popping, when Roland's fat belly bounced her against the glass counter. The inked man angrily eyed Bar Jonah, seeing him shove Roland into his wife.

Bar Jonah walked up to Stanley and asked him if he liked the movie. Stanley apathetically nodded yes. "Let's go," Bar Jonah said. The boys and Bar Jonah walked out the door of the cinema. As Bar Jonah pointed his finger in the direction of the car, he yelled at Stormy to stop running through the parking lot. Glancing back, Roland saw the man with the inked arms coming up fast behind Bar Jonah. Roland elbowed Bar Jonah in the side and told him to look behind him. Bar Jonah stopped and started to turn around.

Just as Bar Jonah was beginning to turn his head, he felt a strong hand push him from behind, causing him to lose his balance. Bar Jonah stumbled and fell into Roland. Roland caught Bar Jonah by the shoulder and pushed him back upright. Suddenly Bar Jonah found himself staring into a pair of seething eyes. Right before Bar Jonah felt the man shove him again, he saw the man's inked arm rapidly gaining momentum towards his right shoulder. When the palm of the man's hand hit Bar Jonah's shoulder, he stumbled and fell down on the pavement. Roland started yelling for the man to leave Bar Jonah alone and took a threatening step toward him. The man stopped, looked at Roland and told him to stay the fuck out of it or he would smack the piss out of him. Roland cowered.

Bar Jonah, pushing himself to his feet, glanced over and saw Stanley holding onto Stormy, crouching in between two parked cars. Right when Bar Jonah straightened up, the inked man backhanded him across the face, causing Bar Jonah's head to snap sideways. Bar Jonah scuffed his elbow when he fell against the rust-peppered fender of a parked car. The man looked down searingly at Bar Jonah and said that a pussy like him wasn't even worth punching. Roland started posturing again as if he was going to do something, but the inked man had been in enough fights to know when someone was bluffing. Bar Jonah's tongue slipped out of his mouth and swiped up the trickle of blood that was running from his nose down over his lip.

The man's wife quietly appeared out of nowhere, watching. Crumbles of red-flecked flaking chrome covered Bar Jonah's hands, after he used the bumper of the car to push himself back to his feet. As Bar Jonah stood up, he slapped his hands together, sending the chrome flakes twinkling in the exiting patrons' bright headlights. As Bar Jonah looked over at the man's wife, he could see that she had a thick black cobra with red eyes crawling up from between her breasts.

Bar Jonah felt the man's hand twist a wad full of his hair on the back of his head, while his other hand grab Bar Jonah's jowls under his stubby chin. The man spun Bar Jonah around to face his wife. Bar Jonah's jaw started moving up and down, like he was supposed to be talking but no words were coming out of his mouth. Then the wife began to laugh out loud, as her husband acted like he was a ventriloquist and Bar Jonah was his dummy. The hand moved Bar Jonah's jaws like a marionette, "I'm a pussy, I'm a pussy, I'm a pussy ..." squeaked out, on a trail of spittle, between the man's clenched teeth. Bar Jonah felt the hair on the back of his head being twisted tighter when he tried to pull away. Roland helplessly watched the spectacle, tears streaming down his cheeks. Finally the man squeezed Bar Jonah's jaw harder between his fingers and made the jaw tell his wife it was sorry for pushing the fat Indian kid into her. Contented, his wife thought Bar Jonah had had enough humiliation. "Let him go," she said. When the man shoved Bar Jonah, he fell and hit the asphalt with a boggy thump. The inked husband and wife and their black cobras turned around and disappeared into the crisscrossing maze of the parking lot. Stanley and Stormy were still standing in between the same two cars. Stanley was smiling.

* * *

In late July, Bar Jonah started making more trips to Canada, Idaho and Washington, hitting toy shows wherever he could. After the incident with Roland and Stanley, Bar Jonah felt satiated. The boys had been like warm clay, so soft and pliable. Bar Jonah had few concerns about the boys telling the secrets of their special times together to anyone. He believed that, especially as time went by, memories would become more faded, especially with three kids who Bar Jonah said were not only retards but Indian retards.

Around early August, Lori thought that it would be a good idea to move from the apartment above Bar Jonah. The boys didn't bother to go back down to Bar Jonah's much, after that last time they'd all gone to the movies. Bar Jonah wasn't as generous as he used to be either with offering to watch the kids or to help her out. So they thought it would be best if they moved on. Stanley had decided that he wanted to move back up to the Fort Peck Indian Reservation with Tanya.

One late afternoon, Bar Jonah knocked at Lori's door to see if Roland wanted to go and get supper. Roland heard Bar Jonah's voice at the door asking Lori if he could go. Almost before Lori could say yes or no, Roland was jumping up and down saying how much he wanted to go. As Bar Jonah and Roland were walking to the car, Roland told Bar Jonah how he sure missed having fun with him. Bar Jonah said he had really missed Roland too. In the car on the way to the restaurant Roland began crying, telling Bar Jonah how he was the only one who had ever wanted to teach him things and didn't think he was a dummy. Bar Jonah told Roland that he was always like a son to him; he was a really good photographer too. It was too bad Roland had decided not to become a Marshal because he sure would have made a good one. Roland said he thought so too, but he didn't want to be shocked anymore, so he probably couldn't get into the Marshals.

Bar Jonah told Roland that he didn't ever want kids to make fun of him, so it was best that Roland never say anything about the time that he had touched Bar Jonah's penis. Bar Jonah said he'd forgiven him and had prayed about it. Now it was time to move on and become friends again. Roland said he was glad because he really wanted to become friends again too. They always had so much fun together. Would it be okay, Roland asked, if just he and Bar Jonah became best friends? Stormy was too young to be able to do the things that he and Bar Jonah liked to do and Stanley was back up on the Res. Bar Jonah said that sounded like a great idea. Stormy got on his nerves too.

When they pulled into the parking lot, Bar Jonah began breathing fast and wiping his forehead with the back of his hand. Roland asked Bar Jonah if he was okay. Bar Jonah said it happened to him every time he pulled into a parking lot now. Roland said he didn't understand. Bar Jonah said that the beating that he took for Roland brought back all of the memories of being raped and attacked by the eight boys when he was a ten year old. But, and most importantly, Bar Jonah told Roland that he forgave him; he was glad to take the beating from the man with the inked arms instead of Roland. That's just what dads do. But Roland had to promise that he wouldn't do any more pushing and shoving in public. Roland got tears in his eyes when he said he would never do anything like that again.

After supper, Bar Jonah said it would make him too nervous to go to a movie after what Roland had put him through. It was best that Stanley had gone back to the reservation. He thought he'd be happier there. Bar Jonah only ever wanted what was best for Stanley and the boys. Roland agreed.

CHAPTER FOUR

Busted

After school started Lori and Gerald were still talking about getting a new place but hadn't done anything about it. They were three months behind on their rent and the landlord was beginning to hound them something awful, always knocking on their door wanting his money. Lori told him he'd get it when she had it.

Late on a Friday night in October, Lori, Gerald and the boys moved into a small pink house not too far from Roland's high school. She didn't leave a forwarding address with anyone except Bar Jonah. Usually they wrote each other about once a week. Bar Jonah didn't get over there much at all. It was too far to drive and he didn't have much money. He was also working more hours at Hardee's. But he sure missed her and the boys. Someday they were going to have to set some time aside to have a big dinner, Bar Jonah wrote.

A couple of months after school started, Bar Jonah began visiting Lincoln Elementary almost exclusively. A couple of the teachers at the other schools commented that they were surprised Bar Jonah hadn't been coming around on patrol. He said that he had been temporarily reassigned but he was back now. One of the teachers joked that Bar Jonah was more predictable than the school clock. When the teacher looked out the window and saw Bar Jonah, she knew her day was almost over.

* * *

Detective Robert Burton lived in the neighborhood of Lincoln Elementary School which sits on the corner of 27th Street and 6th Avenue S. On December 6th, 1999, Detective Burton saw Bar Jonah hanging around the school. He knew Bar Jonah didn't live in the area and was curious why he was walking up and down the sidewalk in such close proximity to Lincoln Elementary.

As Burton was driving to work on December 13th, he again saw Bar Jonah a block away from Lincoln Elementary. Burton called dispatch on his portable radio and told them to send a patrol officer out to investigate a "suspicious male" walking westbound on 5th Avenue in the 2900 block. Bar Jonah was between 29th and 30th streets, but closer to 29th. Burton told dispatch the man was wearing a dark blue police jacket.

A few minutes later, Officer Steve Brunk heard the dispatch and observed the man in question walking in the 400 block of 27th Street S. Brunk drove past the man, made a U-turn and pulled up to the curb. Even though the street lights were on, it was still not possible to get a good look at the man from the patrol car. Brunk switched on his spotlight and shined it on the man's face. Over his loudspeaker, Brunk told the man to walk to the front of his car. The man stopped and turned to look at Brunk. The man fit the description of the suspicious person Detective Burton had called in about.

Brunk got out of his patrol car and walked toward the man. He asked him to identify himself. The man said his name was Nathaniel Bar Jonah. He was wearing a dark blue, nylon police jacket with a reinforced area over the left breast pocket for a police badge. Bar Jonah was standing with his hands inside his jacket pockets. Brunk told Bar Jonah to remove his hands from his pockets. As he was pulling his hands from his pockets Officer Badgley pulled up as backup. Brunk asked Bar Jonah if he was carrying any weapons. Bar Jonah told Brunk he had a stun gun. Badgley then took over and had Bar Jonah lean against his patrol car and began to pat him down. When Badgley checked Bar Jonah's right jacket pocket he found the stun gun. Badgley pulled the stun gun out of Bar Jonah's jacket pocket, pressed the switch on the side and saw the electric blue arc bridge the two shiny metal tits in the early morning darkness. There was also a can of pepper spray in Bar Jonah's left front pant pocket. In his left jacket pocket, there was another can of pepper spray as well as a "Special Investigator" badge. Badgley found a silver toy revolver in Bar Jonah's right pant pocket. Each time Badgley found something, he handed it to Brunk who placed it on the hood of his patrol car. Burton also arrived at the scene within a few minutes of hearing the call for backup. Burton had Badgley put Bar Jonah into Badgley's cruiser while the officers talked among themselves. The question was whether or not carrying a stun gun out of plain view was considered a violation of Montana's concealed carry law. None of the officers could find anything specifically related to this, under Montana statutes. Badgley called his shift commander who told him to make a report. The case would be kicked over to the detective division and the county attorney's office. In the meantime, the shift commander told Badgley to let Bar Jonah go.

At a police officer briefing on the morning of December 15th, Detective Bellusci received notice that Bar Jonah had been in the area of Lincoln Elementary School and had been briefly detained. Bellusci also learned that Bar Jonah was carrying a stun gun, pepper spray, a toy gun, a toy police badge and was dressed in a police jacket. Detective Burton cornered Bellusci after report and told him that he had seen Bar Jonah in the area of Lincoln School a week before Brunk had stopped him on the thirteenth. Bellusci was incensed. From his perspective, the 1994 case should never have been dropped; Bar Jonah should have been sent back to prison. Bellusci remembered that the sexual offender evaluation that was done as part of the '94 case showed that Bar Jonah was at a high risk to reoffend. Later that afternoon, Bellusci contacted Deputy County Attorney Julie Macek and went over the case with her. Macek believed that Bar Jonah should be charged with possession of a concealed weapon and impersonating a police officer. Macek drafted a search warrant for Bellusci's signature and called District Judge Kenneth Neill. Neill signed the warrant without hesitation.

Bellusci believed that Bar Jonah was either planning a kidnapping or was on his way to carry one out that he had already planned. Bellusci was still bitter about the charges against Bar Jonah being dismissed in the Shawn Watkins case. He wasn't about to let it happen again.

At three p.m., Det. Bellusci, Sgt. Reseubauch, Lt. Sinnott, Det. Hollis, Det. Burton, and FBI Agent James Wilson served the search warrant on Bar Jonah. During the search they seized a blue nylon police jacket, a silver toy revolver, one silver badge, a stun gun, a ball cap with the designation "Security Enforcement", two disposable cameras, two albums containing more than 14,000 pictures of children, another coat with a police badge in the right pocket, two packs of undeveloped 35 mm film, plastic baseball card sleeves with pictures of children that hadn't yet been put into the binders, hundreds of loose photographs of children, and one American Junior Workout video tape.

Bellusci also found a piece of paper in a drawer, sitting beside the rope Bar Jonah had used to choke Stanley. On the paper were names run together, printed in black ink. Bellusci had no idea what they meant.

ROLANDBAERNATHYSTORMYA
BERNATHYBARRYFLANNIGAN
ERIKSCHMIDTLOGANHCKSER
IKHATHAWAYNATHANORDJON
NATHANAELBENJAMIN
LEVIBARFJONAHBJNATHA
NNATEDAVIDPAULBROWNDA
VEMICHAELLEONARDJARO
MINSKITAMMYMARIEJAROM
INSKIMANDYLEEJAROMINS
KILOISANNJAROMINSKI
FOSHAYLEEFOSHAYSHAWN
MICHAELWATKINSJULIE
WATKINSSHAWNMICHAELR
OSSINNIKKIRUSSINMISSYRO
SSINZACKERYRAMSEYCHRIS
WESTPHALLMICHAELSURPRIS
EBILLYBENOITALENRICKIASDIED

Wilson found a piece of paper with *Catch A Little Fish And A Little Boy Pops Out* scribbled above a fairy tale Bar Jonah had written entitled *"WHY THE SALMON IS RESPECTED"*. The story read:

> *Once the son of a respected woman took a piece of salmon from the food box without permission. After being scolded, the boy went up river where he sat down and sulked. A voice called to him from a canoe, "Get in!" And in he climbed. The canoe went further up river and came to a village with large houses. The front of the first house was painted with the "qunis" or dog salmon design. Other fine house fronts were painted with the coho, sockeye, steelhead, and spring salmon. In front of the spring salmon house, the mysterious canoe ran ashore, and the people entered, the boy following. "You are in the house of the salmon people," mouse woman said. "You healed the crippled leg of the salmon chief when you took the fish from*

67

your mother's food box. The chief's leg was cured because you straightened the salmon." Of course, the boy was baffled at what mouse woman told him. "The chief brought you here to be properly rewarded. But," the mouse woman warned, "eat none of the food offered, not even what looks like berries, because they are eyes of dead people!" "But I am hungry," complained the boy, "what shall I eat?" "Wait until tomorrow," mouse woman instructed, "then go outside where children, who are really salmon, will be playing. Catch a child, hit him with your club, and eat him. Then you must carefully burn every bone and all the salmon parts that you do not eat." The boy discovered that the child became a real salmon the instant he clubbed it. Satisfying his hunger, the boy burned the bones and returned to the fine house. Suddenly, a child burst through the door screaming, "One of my eyes is gone!" Instantly, mouse woman materialized. "You failed to burn one of the eyes of the salmon. Go find the eye and burn it! Hurry!" When the boy did as instructed, he saw the child's eyes were normal again. Several days later, the salmon child sent the boy to see if the new leaves were on the trees. The seeds were there food. "Far up river the new leaves have budded," the boy reported. "That is good," said the chief. "We go to the seed ground tomorrow." A salmon skin was given to the boy. "Put this on for our journey," the chief ordered. "You will go with us." Diving into the water, the boy discovered the salmon skin enabled him to swim as fast as a salmon. In fact, the young man became a salmon, and with the others, he swam up stream toward the spawning grounds. "See what a huge qunis I have caught," shouted a chief, who was netting salmon in the rapids near his village. "This is the largest I have ever seen." He took the big salmon to his wife. When she cut the great qunis open with her clam shell knife to prepare the feast, she discovered a child in the salmon. From this experience with the supernatural salmon, the people learned to ceremonially burn all the bones and uneaten parts of the first salmon caught in the spring. Thus, the salmon spirits knew that the clan was

*respected and the ceremony became a great event and evolved
into a "new year" ritual in which all of the nature spirits were
involved to assure that all things would be renewed.*

As soon as the search was over, Wilson went back to his office
and wrote a letter to Pat O'Malley, Assistant Records Supervisor at Bridgewater State Hospital.

This letter is to request information regarding David P.
Brown, aka Nathaniel Benjamin Levi Bar Jonah, DOB
02/15/57, 02/15/55, 03/15/57, SSN 026-46-5866, 026-46-
5861. Brown was confined to the Massachusetts Department of Corrections from approximately 1978 through
1991 for kidnapping and attempting to kill two boys in
Shrewsbury, Massachusetts in 1977. Brown lured the
boys into his car by showing an official-looking badge
and stating that he was a police officer and that they
needed to come with him presumably for questioning.
Brown is currently in Great Falls, Montana. On 12/13/99
Brown was questioned by Great Falls police officers as
he walked through a residential area near a city park and
an elementary school. Brown was wearing a police type
jacket, and had a badge, stun gun, two cans of pepper
spray, and a fake gun in his possession. Police were unable to arrest Brown at that time because he had not broken
any laws. The Great Falls resident agency of the Federal
Bureau of Investigation (FBI) is assisting the Great Falls
police department in the investigation of this matter, as
Brown has been identified as a possible suspect in the
disappearance of a ten-year-old boy from Great Falls in
1996. The FBI believes that Brown may have passed the
threshold between fantasy and acting out his fantasies,
therefore time is of the utmost importance. Please review
his prison file for any pertinent information in regards
to official police reports, reports of him developing a
sadistic board game, any statements made by Brown,

and any other items could be significant in regards to Brown's prison experience which could be used by FBI behavioral science profilers to better assess Brown and determine the appropriate method of confronting and questioning him.

Thank you,

James Wilson, Special Agent

* * *

On the morning of December 16th, Bellusci gave the undeveloped film canisters to David Bissonette, who was a lab technician for the GFPD. When Bissonette developed the film, he called Bellusci telling him he had a proof sheet that he should see. There were photographs of young boys playing in what appeared to be the area outside of Bar Jonah's apartment building. There were also photographs of a young Native American boy lying on Bar Jonah's couch with his finger in his mouth and his shirt pulled up. Bellusci thought the photograph looked posed. Another photograph showed a young man, shirtless, who was sleeping on Bar Jonah's loveseat. In between the photographs of the young boys were photographs of Bar Jonah, naked from the waist down, with his penis in different stages of erection. Bellusci recognized one of the young boys in the photographs. He knew the boys had lived in the same apartment building as Bar Jonah. A little after noon on the 16th, Bellusci had tracked down the Big Leggins and asked Lori if she knew Bar Jonah. She said she did and he was a good friend. Lori also said Bar Jonah had taken care of her boys and that he was the best babysitter she'd ever had.

After Bellusci met with Lori, he called Detective Burton and told him to arrest Bar Jonah. The police had been watching Bar Jonah around the clock, since Brunk had stopped him on the 13th. Burton called dispatch to find out Bar Jonah's whereabouts. The duty officer told him Bar Jonah was at the local Job

Service. While Burton drove over to the Job Service building, he called dispatch again and requested a patrol officer meet him there to transport a prisoner. When Burton arrived at the Job Service he found Bar Jonah looking through the job postings on the cork bulletin board, just inside the door. Burton told Bar Jonah that he was placing him under arrest for impersonating a police officer and carrying a concealed weapon. When Burton patted Bar Jonah down he found a can of pepper spray in his right front pants pocket. He also found a piece of paper folded up in Bar Jonah's wallet where nine words were carefully printed,

Hasah	*Caforum*
Minna	*Lecourum*
Rab(bit)	*Plumius*
Deporum	*Alegy*
Mackdum	

Burton told Bar Jonah to put his hands behind his back. Bar Jonah offered no resistance; he did as he was told. The second before Burton clicked the polished stainless steel handcuffs around Bar Jonah's thick wrists would be the last time that he would see the world as a free man.

Digging deeper

After Bellusci saw the photographs, he became concerned that the case against Bar Jonah may be more involved than he initially thought. On the morning of the 17th, Bellusci again went to Macek and requested another search warrant. Judge Neill again issued a search warrant for Bar Jonah's apartment. When Bellusci got to Bar Jonah's and began going through his apartment, he discovered more than twenty boxes of photographs and cutouts from magazines. He also found a rope with a crude noose tied at one end. It would take months to go through everything in the apartment. Bellusci decided to seize what he thought would be necessary for the investigation and have it transported to the police department, where it would be housed in the gymnasium. At one point Bellusci opened Bar Jonah's freezer and found dozens of packages what appeared to be rotted meat. Bellusci said the smell almost knocked him off of his feet. He slammed the freezer door shut without taking any samples. It was something that would haunt him through-out the rest of his career as a police officer.

One of the officers assisting in the search opened a drawer in the kitchen and found dozens of knives. He grabbed a few, bagged them and left maybe fifty behind. The search scene was chaotic. There was no organized rhyme or reason as to the way the search was conducted. Bellusci said he didn't know what they were dealing with and so no specific orders were given about what to look for and how to handle any possible evidence. More than forty boxes were carried out of Bar Jonah's apartment and taken to the police gymnasium. However, there were thousands of items left behind.

* * *

Doc sat at the HiHo tipping back shot after shot, as he watched cop after cop carry box after box out of Bar Jonah's apartment. With each toss of the glass Doc quelled his nervousness about what may be lingering around Bar Jonah's apartment that could somehow tie him to Zach. Doc didn't want to go back to jail. The '94 stint had been hard on him. County jail hadn't been that bad, but being locked up in a prison cage at his age would just wear a man down to the bone.

* * *

Doc always believed love was close at hand. But circumstances too always seemed to be acting upon him, like never ending tidal waves of woes. When Doc was asked to serve his coun-try in the Korean War, he faced the ongoing possibility of extinction, with day-in and day-out onslaughts of those little sawed-off, slant-eyed bastards coming at him, one right after the other. And now, as Doc increasingly needed his cane for more than just a prop, his heart had begun playing an unco-ordinated hopscotch in his chest. But still, he only longed for one thing. Doc knew that to again find love would make his disharmonious heart quiver with melodious rapture. If Doc were locked away, the fire steeping the anguish of his loneli-ness would never be extinguished.

Clean up

The first phone call that Bar Jonah made when he was booked into the Cascade County Jail was to Tyra. He told her what he had been charged with and about the cops searching his apart-ment, twice. Tyra wanted to know what the cops were look-ing for. Even to Tyra, it seemed like they were going to a lot of trouble for a concealed weapons and impersonating charge. Bar Jonah said he had no idea but thought it would be a good idea if she and Bob went in and cleaned out the apartment. Get rid of everything. He especially wanted the meat in his refrigerator thrown out. They should scrub everything down too. Use bleach water.

That night Bob called Lori and told her he wanted Roland to help him and Tyra clean out Bar Jonah's apartment. Bar Jonah had been arrested and he didn't want him to get stuck with having to pay rent on a place where he wasn't living. Lori said sure, she understood. Lori was really upset that Bar Jonah had been arrested. She wanted to know if there was anything she could do. Bob told her the cops would probably be coming by to question her. If they did, she should keep her mouth shut. Lori said that some cop named "Bellus" something or other had already come by. But she told him Bar Jonah was a nice guy and a good babysitter. "Bellus" wanted to know if Bar Jonah had ever done anything to her boys, like touching them in some kind of sexual way. Lori told Bob she told the cop that she didn't know nothin' about Bar Jonah ever touching her kids in a bad way. "Bar Jonah was a real good man," she said. Bob also told her that if she said anything it could bring the social service people down around her neck for leaving the kids alone so much and having Bar Jonah take care of them. Lori reassured Bob she sure wouldn't say nothin'.

* * *

On the morning of December 18th, Bob and Tyra arrived at Bar Jonah's apartment about nine a.m. Lori had already dropped off Roland. He was running up and down the stairs just like he used to. He had been at the top of the stairs when he heard Bob's truck pull up. As Roland jumped down the stairs, he took the last three in one long leap. Roland's feet landed with a prideful plunk, squarely in between the rusted nail heads poking through the seemingly always wet, warped plywood landing.

As soon as Roland walked out of the stairwell, Bob reached out to shake his hand. While holding tightly onto Roland's limp hand, Bob told him that if the cops came around it was going to be important for him to say only good things about Bar Jonah. Other than that, he should keep his mouth shut. Bob didn't want Roland to have to feel guilty for saying something to the cops that would send Bar Jonah back to prison for life. Mostly Bob told Roland that he was worried that the police and family services might start investigating Lori and end up putting Roland and Stormy in foster care. If family services took the kids away, they'd probably never get to see their mom again, Bob said. It was really important that Roland keep his mouth shut. Roland said he understood, he wouldn't say nothing to no one.

When they got into Bar Jonah's apartment, Roland asked Bob and Tyra what he should save. He wasn't sure what Bar Jonah wanted to keep, since he had so much stuff. Bob told

Roland to throw out everything. *Nothing* was to be left behind in the apartment. There was a big dumpster outside. Put everything in there, Tyra said. In a few hours the green dumpster was completely filled. Bob wore bright yellow rubber gloves when he got the meat out of the freezer and stuffed it into a couple of doubled up grocery bags. He cleared a space in the middle of all of Bar Jonah's writings, Christmas ornaments, pictures, clothes, cookbooks and toys that they had thrown into the dumpster and shoved the bags of meat deep into the crevasse. Then Bob pulled the other garbage back on top of the bags of meat. The knives were strewn about randomly, intermingling with the rest of the junk. After they got everything out of the apartment, Bob and Tyra scrubbed the place down with bleach water. He told Roland he wanted to make sure Bar Jonah got his deposit back.

* * *

On Christmas Eve the Cascade County Jail woke up about six a.m. The clanging echo of cell doors opening and sounds of prisoners belching and farting filled the tiled concrete corridors. Bar Jonah had been awake since about five composing the letters in his head that he had to write that day. After a breakfast of two over-easy elastic eggs with anemic pale yellow yolks, one piece of flat fat bacon, two pieces of cold toast with some kind of mixed fruit jelly and a cup of lukewarm see-through coffee, Bar Jonah began to put his thoughts to paper.

> *"Dear Lori, I am facing 10 years in prison and I want you to help me out. I want you to write a letter to the prosecutor's office on my behalf. You can tell them all that I have done for you and I have done a lot. You can return the favor to me now."*

Bar Jonah then wrote a special letter to Stormy. He called him *"G-Man"* in the letter. *"I miss you so much,"* Bar Jonah wrote. *"I want you to draw a picture for me that I can hang on the wall of my cell, until I get out of here."* Before handing the letters to the guard to mail, Bar Jonah drew a unicorn on the envelope addressed to Lori and a little teddy bear, wrapped in a heart on Stormy's envelope. Bar Jonah knew Stormy loved teddy bears. He would think it was pretty special seeing a teddy on the envelope first thing.

Bar Jonah was sitting on his bunk when one of the guards came by, stopping outside of Bar Jonah's cell. The guard had a clipboard and seemed to be completing some kind of checklist. He was standing with his profile to Bar Jonah. Bar Jonah leaned forward on his bunk and fixed his eyes on the guard. By the barely perceptible movements of the guard's lips and eyelashes, Bar Jonah knew the guard had felt his gaze. The guard did not turn to face Bar Jonah, but his highly starched dark gray collar stirred and rose high to brush the bottom of his small pink flushed ears. Then the guard shrugged his shoulders, as though he were shaking something unbeknownst to him off of his back and walked away, curiously turning his head from side to side.

CHAPTER FIVE

The distraction

Shirley Klesh decided to do some shopping in Minneapolis, after she had gone from Great Falls back to the Midwest to visit her family. As she was paying for a pair of red pumps, she noticed a credit card application hawking an interest rate that looked too good to resist. Before she left the store Shirley penned in her address, 2405 7th St South, Great Falls, Montana along with her date of birth and social security number. When she left the store the cold winds blowing in from the north reminded her of central Montana. For early September, they seemed particularly bitter though. There was a mailbox sitting on the curb. In one nice move, she pulled down the squeaky blue door of the mailbox and tossed the credit card application inside without ever missing a step. The wind was so biting that she didn't even pull the door back down to see if her application had slid down the chute to mingle with the rest of the mail. Fortunately, or not, it had. On September 14th credit card #4072591004508845, with the fabulous interest rate, was delivered just a few blocks away to 2405 4th St South: the home of Great Falls Police Lieutenant Greg Church. Church was off duty the day the card arrived. He planned to spend most of the day at one of the local casinos. He spit polished himself thinking he might also not have to spend the night alone, especially if he hit the big money. Women in the casinos always hung around waiting for a man to win big. Toss them a smile and a few bucks and they'll hop in your bed pretty quick. Church drove through the back streets thinking about what he was going to do with the money he was planning to win. Keno was a good game but they had craps in one of the back rooms. Live betting with no limit. He could pull down some good winnings. He could feel it.

The Keno wasn't any good. Something was wrong with the machine, Church kept complaining to the bar hop, who wandered around handing out free beer and cheap wine to the steady players. He'd just cashed his check. Church had over a thousand in fifties rolled up and stuffed in his cop blue jacket pocket. The bar hop came over, handed Church a beer and lamented with him about the bad luck he was having with the machine. "Fuck," Church railed as he pounded his fist on the machine. The bar hop stayed with Church, even rubbing his tense back a few times to try to help him out. It wasn't doing any good though. He slipped a twenty into the waist of the bar hop's hip huggers and quietly told her to take him to where the real action was. Craps was his game.

* * *

The back room looked more like a garage quickly flipped into a makeshift casino. A couple of poker tables and a long, home-made craps table took up most of the room. Hot sweat and stale beer stunk the place up. Smoke hung thick around the low-hanging cone-shaped lights. The table was high stakes. A couple of players from out of town were tossing money around and winning pretty good. Church stood by for a few minutes rubbing his fingertips over the wad of cash bulging in his pocket, like a canker sore that won't let your tongue alone. How much to get in, Church yelled. The man with the rake yelled back five hundred. Church pulled out the wad and peeled off ten fifties.

He slapped it down on a 10:1 bet, took the dice, shook them around in his wet palm and called for his "darling be good to me" rolling for a seven. The dice bounced off the far end of the table, popped into the air and fell onto the cheap green velvet. One die spun around for half-a-second on a barely noticeable smoothed off corner. Before the die dropped, Church reached out ready to sweep the table of its cash. He knew he'd won big. Another hand reached out and grabbed his wrist. "It's three, fucker, you rolled a three. You lose." The hand let go of Church's wrist and shoved the cash down the table. The man with the rake yelled, "Five thousand owed the table." Church turned white. He had just a bit more than five hundred left and he owed the house five big ones.

Church knew his luck was going to turn with this bet. He'd never been more sure. Even the other times when he lost big. Lots of reasons, especially that night when he had slipped and let the dice go before he meant to. But that had only been a few hundred. He'd never even been close to losing five thousand before. "All or nothing, five hundred, 10:1, rolling for 11." Church screamed so loud that the smoke clinging to the bare bulb, hanging from a frayed cord, began to scatter and look for other light. Again Church tossed the dice around in his shooting hand. Sensuously he closed his eyes and whispered softly to his closed palm, "Come on darling, don't hold back on me baby, give it to daddy …" Church pulled his fist to his lips, kissed his callused knobby knuckles and sent the dice flying down the table.

As soon as the dice left Church's clenched hand they smacked into each other in midair, then went flying to either side of the table falling to a six and one. Church stared down the table looking like a bowler who'd just missed the perfect 300, had it not been for the split pins staring back at him from the end of the lane. "Seven," the man with the rake dispassionately yelled. "Five thousand owed the table." A thick fat finger reached out and touched Church's shoulder. Church heard someone say that he needed to pay the house. He didn't have that kind of money, he said back. The big man suggested that they go outside and talk. It was best not to upset the other customers, he said. In the alley, the man told Church he needs to pay up to the house, then he can go back in and play some more. Church said he's tapped. He said again he doesn't have that kind of money. He's busted. The man told Church they have a serious problem and need to come to some kind of solution. Church reached into his back pocket and flipped out his gold detective shield and threatened to push back hard if the man doesn't see it his way. The man pushed Church into the gray cinder block wall and said he's not worried. It doesn't matter to him if the shield is gold or silver. Church owes the money and he's going to pay it, one way or another. The man knows who Church is. He knows who his family is too. He would hate for Church's family to get brought into something they didn't have nothin' to do with. Before the man walked away, he leaned close to Church's face and told him he has twenty-four hours. Ten thousand dollars in cash. No time extended, no warnings, nothing, twenty-four hours.

No one ever found out how Church paid the house the ten grand. It was one of the few unsolved mysteries of his life. He would never talk about it. It was known that Church took a lot of time off over the next couple of weeks and laid low.

Church had to get away. He needed a break. It was just getting too hot around Great Falls and he was under a lot of pressure. He had, however, been able to get the loan shark paid off. There were rumors that his old man, who always seemed to be getting him out of scrapes and jams, put up the cash in order to keep his boy from taking a beating and maybe him too.

On September 20th, Church tried to activate Shirley Klesh's credit card that had mistakenly been delivered to his house. He had decided he was going to show his new girlfriend a good time and take her to Vegas for the weekend. His luck would be better there. Church called from his home phone, to activate the credit card. It didn't work. The damn company wanted Church to key in Klesh's date of birth and social security number in order to activate the card. He didn't have them. It pissed him off so bad that he ripped his phone cord out of the wall. Everything had been planned. Now he was going to have to fucking change his plans to go to Vegas with his old lady. She couldn't get any more time off from work till the 8th of October.

On the morning of the 8th, just before they were ready to pull out of the driveway, Church called again to activate the credit card. This time it was successful. It hadn't been a problem for Church to search the Department of Motor Vehicles' records to get Klesh's date of birth and social security number. He slammed down the receiver when the recording offering "special fraud protection" started to play. On the way out of town, Church pulled into a drive-through ATM on 10th Avenue South and at exactly 13:35:30 took $400 in cash against the card. The transaction was videotaped.

A couple of months later, responsible Shirley Klesh was shocked when she began getting nasty calls from the credit card collection department. She didn't have an account with that bank, she said. But, they countered, she had sent in an application back in September. She never received the card and had forgot even sending in for the special offer. On January 6th, 1999, Shirley got a call from the bank's fraud division. Exactly one week later, on the 19th, the case was referred to the Great Falls Police Department, Detective Division for further investigation. Bellusci got assigned the case.

It didn't take Bellusci long to figure out that the address where the card was sent belonged to Lt. Greg Church, one of GFPD's own and one of the most decorated. The card had been activated from his home phone. Bellusci believed that it must have been Church's girlfriend.

Bellusci interviewed Church's girlfriend on January 20th, 1999. According to the girlfriend, "Bellusci sat up close beside me on the couch" and said "Are you afraid of cops?" She also

81

made allegations that Bellusci made other comments to her that were not "professional." At the conclusion of the interview, Church's girlfriend said Bellusci told her "not to tell anyone about the case, not even your father." When Bellusci ended the interview, he asked Church's girlfriend to come down to the station later that day to be fingerprinted, photographed and "further questioned." The girlfriend told him she would. A few hours later she called Bellusci and told him she had retained counsel.

After Bellusci left the girlfriend's house, he called the bank investigator he had been dealing with and told him that he was going to be arresting Church's girlfriend. She was the primary suspect. The bank investigator's notes read that the Great Falls Police Department "will be issuing a warrant for her arrest ... knows where she is located. Needs nothing else from me at this time. Closing case ... asked detective Bellusci to keep me updated."

One of the local bank investigators reviewed the video recording of the transaction. She put a note on the videotape that said "Klesh, 10/8/98, 13:33:13," indicating the time just before Greg Church pulled up to the ATM and stole the $400. The bank investigator even cued up the tape, right before she gave it to Bellusci, to the seconds before Church drove up to the ATM. She thought it would make it easier for Bellusci to iden- tify the suspect, smiling up at the camera, as he took the pressed fresh cash that was being spit out of the machine. However, for some reason, Bellusci did not see Church when he played the cued up videotape and pressed the PLAY button.

* * *

Doris Kimmerle met Greg Church one night in June 1994, when they both happened to be out drinking. Kimmerle is a smart, beautiful brunette and one of the top female bowlers in the country. It didn't take long before they were an "item." Kimmerle had grown up in Great Falls and seemed to know everyone. She had been a beauty queen and known around town as being "as honest as the day is long." A lot of people said they couldn't understand what she was doing with a loser like Church. Shortly after they began dating, Church began to lay down the law. Kimmerle could no longer drive herself to work; he would drive her. She couldn't go out with friends unless he was with her, and she had to stop looking at the "cowboys" when they came into a bar they happened to be frequenting, even if it was just a glance. Kimmerle was to keep her eyes on Church at all times. There were several occasions when Kimmerle defied Church and went out with a few of her friends after work. Church would drive past her house, see that she wasn't home when she was supposed to be and then begin driving around looking for her truck. When he found it, Church would storm into the establishment and cause a scene, demanding that Kimmerle get home. He was always in his cruiser and uniform. Nobody really would mess with him or speak up on her behalf. Other times, when Kimmerle violated "Church's law," she would come home and find holes punched in her walls and her furniture broken. "Don't you fuck with me," Church would scream, Kimmerle said. In early 1996, after "two years of hell," Kimmerle began "secretly" talking to one of her girl-friends on the telephone, about how to leave Church, safely. She just couldn't take his violence anymore. "He's crazy," she said. Kimmerle had also just discovered that Church was more than $40,000 in debt. The more Kimmerle talked to her girlfriend, the more erratic Church became. Church was now beginning to confront Kimmerle about the exact same things she was telling her girlfriend. Sometimes, word for word. She couldn't help but ask herself if her girlfriend was betraying her. Then Kimmerle began to think more sinister thoughts.

Kimmerle began looking around her house for a recording device. It didn't take long until she flipped back the paisley duvet that covered her bed and found, tucked behind a shoe caddy, a small tape recorder wired into her phone line. On the back of the recorder was a sticker that read, "Property of the Great Falls Police Department." Church was incredulous when Kimmerle confronted him. But he was dumbstruck when she said she had had enough and walked out that same afternoon. Kimmerle went directly to Chief Jones. She told him about the recorder. Her purpose was not to get Church into trouble, but to get him help. All of the cops knew he was out of control. He had to be helped before he hurt someone or himself. She also wanted to make sure that someone in the PD knew that she had left Church, in case something happened to her. Kimmerle was scared and stated that "The chief was completely disinterested and said he could do nothing." It didn't take long for Church to get another girlfriend. He though continued to stalk Kimmerle for years.

Right when Bellusci was starting his investigation, Kimmerle decided that she was finally in a financial position where she could buy a new car. Her credit was "flawless," or so she thought. Kimmerle went to a local car lot and found the "perfect car" that she could afford with her "flawless credit." But, when the long-faced, smoking car salesman ran her credit report he wanted to know why she had defaulted on an $11,651 credit card loan, back in March 1996, right before she had left Church.

Kimmerle sat in disbelief. One month before Kimmerle broke up with Church, he had intercepted a credit card application meant for her and completed it with her personal information. But, he used his address. More than three years after she had broken up with Church, he had come back to haunt her. Kimmerle knew that she couldn't go to the GFPD. Instead she went to a friend who was an attorney. Together they contacted the Secret Service. Now the Feds were involved. There were two separate investigations going on of Church at the same time. When Kimmerle met with the Secret Service, she was told that it was good that she had not gone to the PD. Church had a "close personal relationship with one of the department's captains," the agent told Kimmerle.

Church and his direct supervisor, Captain Renman had attended a lot of hot tub parties together. It was well understood in the law enforcement community that Church was a dirty cop. A few weeks later, the Secret Service went to Kimmerle and asked her to work with them to entrap Church into incriminating himself. When the agent came to her house, he brought a tape recorder to hook up to her phone to get any incriminating statements Church might make during the call with Kimmerle. For an hour the Secret Service agent tried to get his equipment to work. There was something wrong with it. It wasn't going to record. They would have to do the call another day. Kimmerle suddenly remembered something. She excused herself and went into her bedroom. "Here," Kimmerle said, "use this," handing the agent a small tape recorder with the words "Property of the Great Falls Police Department" stamped on the back.

Church's "Yeah baby, I'm going to take care of that next week, yeah I've been meaning to take care of that … I'm gonna get that paid back first thing next week" and other empty apologies were recorded on the same recorder he had used to try to entrap Kimmerle. The only difference was that she hadn't done anything wrong.

* * *

Sgt. John Cameron was the detective division shift commander; Renman was his captain. He was starting to hear rumors floating around the department that Lieutenant Church may have been involved in a theft. He knew he had a gambling problem and seemed to always be hungry for money. Cameron went to Renman and said he thought Church was dirty. It needed to be looked into, he said. Renman told Cameron to back off; he would handle it.

The next morning, Great Falls City Manager John Lawton looked up from his desk and saw Cameron standing in his office. "There is a problem," Cameron said as he began to lay out what he believed was a cover-up in the Great Falls Police Department.

About the same time, the Secret Service agent had retrieved a copy of the videotape and was reviewing it back at his office. When the agent scrolled the videotape to the day and time of the withdrawal he froze the screen and printed a picture of Lieutenant Greg Church's face.

* * *

On the afternoon of October 27th, the Secret Service showed up at Church's home and arrested him for bank fraud. A few hours later, Chief Robert Jones received a call from Bellusci telling him that Church had been arrested and charged with a federal crime. There is going to be a "fall-out over this one," Jones said. Jones called Lawton and told him that Church had been picked up. Lawton told Jones he wanted to see him and Renman. A short time later the three men met behind closed doors in Lawton's office. Lawton told Jones he was going to appoint a special Police Inquiry Panel to investigate what had happened. There were going to be questions and Lawton wanted answers. Jones suggested that retired Secret Service agent Leroy "Lee" Scott be asked to head up the panel. Lawton agreed and told Jones to contact Scott.

* * *

Lee Scott spent the first four years of his career in Naval Intelligence. The next thirty he spent with the Secret Service. Four years of that he spent at the White House serving President George H. W. Bush. Scott was also the Special Agent in charge of President Ronald Reagan's Protective Detail. He was soft spoken, insightful and above reproach. Scott was also a highly trained investigator. Before he retired, Scott worked out of the

Great Falls office. He knew all the cops, having worked with them on many investigations. When Scott retired in 1998, he thought it was going to be a life of golf and leisure. It was, until he reluctantly agreed to chair the investigative panel.

When Jones got back to his office he called Scott and explained that Church had been arrested and Lawton had decided to appoint a special committee to investigate the police department. There were going to be accusations of a cover-up. But, Jones assured Scott, no cover-up had occurred. Jones also told Scott that if he accepted, he could "handpick the other members of the panel." Scott took a couple of days to think about it and finally agreed to take on the assignment. But, Scott told Jones that he would accept *no* money. He had to be assured that he would be held harmless, regardless of the findings of his investigation and that he would have free rein. Where the investigation led was where Scott was going. Jones called Lawton and told him Scott's terms. Lawton agreed.

* * *

At the November 16th Commission meeting, Lawton announced that he had appointed a panel to investigate the mishandling of the Church incident and any possibility of a cover-up in the Great Falls Police Department. Lawton said, "To insure an unfettered and thorough investigation, it was deemed necessary to hold harmless, indemnify and defend the members of the inquiry panel of any and all claims, demands or liability arising out of such investigation."

Scott called Jones and gave him a list of names that he was planning to recruit for the panel. He said they were out-standing men that he had worked with in the past. Top notch investigators. "Jones said no to every one of my recommen-dations," Scott said. Jones had changed his mind, *he* would make the appointments, that was best. The other members of the panel Jones chose were Jim Oberhofer and Bert Fairclough. Scott knew Oberhofer was the former Chief of the Missoula,

Montana police department and a very close friend of Jones. Oberhofer had retired to Great Falls after he left the Missoula PD. Fairclough was a local attorney who was struggling with lung cancer. Scott didn't expect Fairclough would be doing much more than lending his name to the investigation.

Scott said he thought that Jones picked him because Jones believed that Scott would play ball with him and keep his mouth shut about any improprieties he found. Scott said he couldn't prove it but that was his sense. He also believed that Jones chose Oberhofer because they were close friends and he could keep an eye on what Scott was doing from the inside. Fairclough was supposed to act as the legal voice of the panel.

* * *

The first person Scott interviewed was Bellusci. Scott said he found Bellusci to be arrogant and cocky and said that Bellusci spent most of his time during the interview smirking when Scott asked him a question. He also thought Belluscihad a poor record of follow-through. According to Scott, the first words out of Bellusci's mouth were "Let's get right to it—there was no cover-up."

Scott was angry. He said, "Bellusci had all the cards, he knew exactly what had happened and then went directly to Renman. He had the whole damn picture and he didn't do anything about it. Nothing except try to keep it quiet and protect Church." Scott said he had the impression that Bellusci thought he was untouchable. During the interview with Scott, Bellusci admitted that he filed an "incomplete criminal report," alleging not with the intent to "cover-up" Church's crime but to throw Church "off track" about the nature of the investigation. Bellusci told Scott that he hoped he could return to the case at a later time when more evidence of Church's guilt came to the surface. Then, Bellusci said, he would be able to arrest him. Scott said, "Bellusci claimed he was not attempting to hide the fact that he basically closed the case." Bellusci said no one ever asked him about the case again. He also said that Renman and Church had a very close relationship and that they "may have been blinded by the case." When Bellusci wrote his only report on the case, he said he made it purposely vague, because he believed that Church was guilty. But, Bellusci said, his superiors didn't agree with him. Bellusci reiterated that he wanted to throw Church off track if he ever saw the report. He also didn't remember ever telling the bank investigator that he was planning on arresting Church's girlfriend. Scott wrote in his report that Bellusci "failed to produce sufficient reasons for his obvious deception."

When Scott interviewed Church, he said that Bellusci had approached him in the coffee room at the PD and said, "I know you did it, I've seen your picture on the videotape. Why don't you admit it?" Church told Scott he was stunned by Bellusci's disclosure and could say nothing to deny his guilt. He did however think that he would soon be arrested. When Church was interviewed on videotape, he again repeated his allegation that Bellusci had told him that he had seen him on the videotape. When Scott confronted Bellusci with Church's allegation, Bellusci said Church was lying and he would "take a polygraph on that."

Shortly after Scott interviewed Bellusci, he received a call from John Cameron. Cameron told Scott that he received a call from Bellusci, right when he began investigating Church. Bellusci wanted to meet Cameron behind the "M&H gas station." Cameron said that Bellusci pulled up beside his car, got out and climbed into Cameron's. Bellusci threw his head back against the head rest and cupped his cheeks with his open palms. "This is the worse day of my life," Bellusci said. He believed that he was going to be made a "scapegoat in this Church mess." One of the lieutenants in the Detective Division was trying to "intimidate" him into keeping his mouth shut. According to Cameron, Bellusci said that he told the chief that

"Church was the suspect on five separate occasions!" It was a short conversation. Cameron listened and advised Bellusci to take the "high road." "Go where the evidence takes you." Bellusci thanked Cameron, got out, climbed back in his car and drove away.

* * *

The agreement between the panel members was that any information discovered during the investigation would remain confidential until the final report was written. But Jones kept calling Scott asking him questions about information that was clearly coming out in the investigation. The only person Scott had discussed the details of the investigation with was Oberhofer. Scott became convinced that Oberhofer was telling Jones everything they talked about. After a few weeks Scott stopped telling Oberhofer anything.

Fairclough remained almost completely uninvolved in the investigation. With his health becoming increasingly compromised, Fairclough's depression about his medical condition was consuming so much of his energy that he didn't participate in any of the panel meetings. Even though each member of the panel was to conduct their own independent investigation, Scott was the only one who actually did. The more aggressive Scott became in his investigation, the more Jones, Renman and Bellusci began to stonewall him. He knew he'd get more cooperation if he kept his mouth shut, but there was absolutely no doubt in Scott's mind that a cover-up had taken place.

Scott was convinced that Bellusci had told Renman that he saw Church on the bank security video. He was also convinced that Renman went straight to Chief Jones. The decision was made, according to Scott, by Jones, Renman and Bellusci to protect Church. Scott was appalled by the attitudes of the three officers. He had been a Secret Service agent for thirty years. Trained to throw himself in front of a bullet intended for the president of the United States, Scott wasn't about to cover up anything.

* * *

Church pled guilty in federal court to grand theft. He was going to federal prison in Oregon. Before sentencing, Scott again met with Church at his attorney's office and told him that if he would be willing to wear a wire and entrap Jones, Renman and Bellusci, he would be willing to speak at his sentencing about his cooperation and assistance. Church agreed. Church would call and ask for a meeting with Jones, Renman and Bellusci. He was going to say that he needed their help at sentencing. Church was also going to say that he had kept his mouth shut about their part in the cover-up and now it was time to help him out.

Church called Jones and told him he wanted to meet with him, Renman and Bellusci. "Set it up," he said. On the morning of the meeting Church was to meet Scott, who had gotten a wire rig from the FBI. Scott was going to put the wire on Church right before he went to the PD for the meeting. Scott would be close by, listening and recording the conversations. If any of them incriminated themselves, Scott was going to recommend indictments for obstruction.

Scott was supposed to meet with Church at ten a.m. Church didn't show. About eleven Scott got a call from Church's attorney. Church had decided it was not in his best interest to go ahead with the meeting. Church was sentenced to five months.

* * *

Three weeks before Scott completed the final report, Fairclough's wife came home for lunch and found him hanging in the garage. He wasn't going to survive the lung cancer anyway. What was the point of putting his family through any more agony? Cameron said he was the duty sargeant when the suicide call came in. He left the station and headed up to Fairclough's house. As he was driving, Cameron heard Renman come on the radio and say "69 Renman, I'm heading up there." Cameron thought it was strange that Renman was going to the scene because he knew that Fairclough was part of the investigative panel. When Cameron arrived at the scene Renman was already there. Cameron went into the garage. They hadn't cut Fairclough down yet. He was just hanging there, his neck stretched, his head black. Renman walked into the garage and then disappeared into the house. Cameron said he thought he was looking for anything that might tell him what Fairclough was going to recommend. He didn't find anything. There was nothing there. Scott hadn't told either Fairclough or Oberhofer what his recommendations were going to be. When Renman came back out into the garage, Cameron said he seemed to be taking voyeuristic delight at seeing Fairclough hanging from the rafter.

* * *

On January 19th, 2000, Great Falls mayor Randy Gray called a special city commission meeting. When Scott arrived at the meeting, Jones was waiting in the lobby for him. "If you can cut me some slack on this, I'll quit in three months," Jones said to Scott. He only had a few more months until retirement. Jones just needed a little more time. Scott said he looked incredulously at Jones. After the mayor called the meeting to order, he turned it over to John Lawton who explained that he wanted to discuss the final report submitted to his office by the Police Inquiry Panel. He also said that the city was obligated to go into executive session to discuss employee disciplinary matters, which would remain confidential. Gray called for the meeting to be closed at 4:41 and it was reconvened as an open meeting at 5:19.

Lawton reported that he had set the Police Inquiry Panel to address three primary questions. Was there a deliberate cover-up of any aspect of the allegations against Church by any member of the Great Falls Police Department? What were the specific shortcomings of the investigation of Church by the GFPD. And, what were their causes? Lawton also wanted to know what changes in the policies, procedures and operations of the GFPD should be made to prevent any similar problems from occurring in the future. Even though Lawton knew better, he said that each member of the panel had conducted their own investigation and that a final report had been compiled from their findings. Oberhofer was at the meeting too.

Lawton said that, by definition, a cover-up is considered to be "an intentional act or omission to act, committed in concert or alone, by any member of the Great Falls Police Department, to knowingly or purposefully conceal or suppress the acquisition of information related to Church's activity." After reviewing the reports, Lawton concluded "that there was no cover-up by any member of the GFPD." But, he further concluded, that various members of the police department could not be held blameless. Lawton added that "When a public employee, particularly at management level, was suspected of wrongdoing, criminal or otherwise, it was incumbent on management at all levels to act with the utmost seriousness and to move with all possible speed to exonerate or confirm the wrongdoing and effectuate appropriate ramifications. Although this matter involved possible theft and deceit by a lieutenant in the police department, the matter was treated as a low priority financial crime and then it was botched at every turn and at every level." Lawton went on to say that "If the proper parties paid attention and treated the investigation more seriously, Mr. Church's criminal activity would have been discovered and Church would have been brought to justice sooner." Scott was furious. He had known Lawton for a long time and believed that he would do the right thing. Scott believed that Lawton would expose the circumstances for what they were and acknowledge that the evidence that Scott had compiled pointed to a *clear* cover-up. He said that he and Lawton never spoke again after the commission meeting.

Lawton said he saw two problems that had emerged from the report. The first was a poor job of investigation and report writing by Bellusci. He also said that there clearly needed to be changes to policy and the way police officers were trained. The other problem was a failure at the command level to fully investigate the matter when it was brought to their attention. Lawton said that Chief Robert Jones would be reprimanded and the reprimand would be placed in his permanent file. Chief Jones would also be instructed to implement systematic changes in the organizational structure of the police department, management training and intradepartmental communications. Lawton didn't mention that the council, while in executive session, had decided that Renman would be terminated.

The Great Falls Police Department had to clean itself up. In essence it had to rebuild itself. Mayor Gray spoke up and said the core issue ultimately was a matter of public trust. Gray looked at Lawton in the meeting and point blank asked him why the public should still have any trust in the police department. Lawton countered that only a few officers were involved in the incident and they came forward once the investigation began and acknowledged their mistakes. He also said that the officers of the GFPD were of the utmost quality and in fact deserved the public's trust. The meeting was adjourned at 6:04 p.m.

* * *

In addition to terminating Renman, the council had also decided that Bellusci would be stripped of his gold detective shield and busted back to patrol duty. It was a hard pill for

94

Bellusci to swallow, but given the circumstances of the case, at least he still had a job. Robert Jones was set up for retirement and in three months he took his gold watch, dedication to service plaque, pension and left his position as chief.

When Scott learned that Renman had been terminated, he said he gave Renman two years and then he bet that Renman would file suit against the city for wrongful termination. Two years, almost to the day, from his termination, Renman filed a wrongful termination suit against the city of Great Falls. But Renman filed the suit in an adjacent Montana city just north of Great Falls, Havre. The hearing took place in a district judge's chambers without the benefit of jury or open proceedings. Great Falls settled with Renman, agreeing to pay him $188,000. A few months later, Renman got a job as a supervisor, investigating illegal gambling operations for the state. The filings and proceedings of the suit remain closed to public scrutiny. There were allegations of other settlements but those records also remain sealed.

In Scott's final report, he stated that "Panel member Jim Oberhofer declined to sign the document at hand, because he was not wholly personally involved in the investigation. He has been encouraged to write a report setting forth his opinion. Therefore any reference to the word 'Panel' within this report should be disregarded." Scott followed with his response to Question 1, "Was there a deliberate cover-up?" He wrote, "Insufficient evidence exists to definitely conclude that there was a cover-up by anyone in this case. But the lay person's examination of the facts established in this case and their comparison with the standard dictionary meaning of the work 'cover-up,' as well as applying common sense to the facts discovered, does support a finding of cover-up. The only other possible explanations which one could draw from the circumstances determined from this investigation is that these officers are either totally incompetent at their profession, innately incapable of drawing reasonable conclusions from known facts, or they are merely unintelligent individuals. In fact, evidence of their professional achievements would lead us to believe them to be the 'best and the brightest' in the Great Falls Police Department."

The Church investigation *consumed* Bellusci and the Great Falls Police Department, taking them away from the time needed to fully investigate the Bar Jonah case.

From the time that Bar Jonah was arrested on December 15th, 1999, until February 2000, his case sat. Even though the city commission had met in November, Bellusci's demotion would not take effect until March 2000. Wilson however continued to investigate, primarily making requests for information on Bar Jonah's background through Bridgewater.

Bar Jonah "mugging" for the camera, wearing his U.S. Marshall T-shirt.

Bar Jonah holding a child.

Police photo of Bar Jonah posing as a police office.

Photo of an unknown boy in Bar Jonah's apartment.

Tyra's white Toyota Corolla.

Young man lying on Bar Jonah's love seat.

Bar Jonah at approximately eighteen.

Bar Jonah's Montana driver's license was renewed on Valentine's Day 1996.

Bar Jonah's rental car.

Aged photo of Zach Ramsey.

CHAPTER SIX

John Cameron

John Cameron was born in Duluth, Minnesota and graduated from high school there in 1979. He is a handsome man, about six foot tall and 170 pounds. Cameron looks like someone that didn't have any hair at birth and never got any as he grew up. He entered the police academy right out of high school and moved to Montana in early 1981, to accept a position as a patrol officer with the Great Falls Police Department.

His first partner, who was "crusty and ugly," had been laying his tracks around the city for thirty years. On his first day on the job, Cameron and his partner were called to a disturbance when an altercation developed. The assailant pulled a gun on Cameron's partner. His partner who was quicker on the draw, drew his .357 and "blew the guy's arm clean off." Cameron stood watching the guy roll around on the ground with blood spurting out of the socket where his arm had been, wondering what the hell he had gotten himself into. In 1989 Cameron got his detective shield and in '94 he was made sergeant. He went back to patrol duty while still having the responsibility of managing sixteen other detectives. In 1997, Cameron was pulled back inside to start the new cold case division. A couple of years later he was put back out as sergeant on patrol again. He was named officer of the year three times and recognized as a "Top Cop" nationally. In February 2000, Detective Sergeant John Cameron was again brought "inside" to take command of the investigation of Bar Jonah.

* * *

For Detective Sgt. John Cameron, who Secret Service Agent Lee Scott referred to as "one of the best investigators I ever worked with," the Bar Jonah case would become a nightmare-ridden obsession. One that would play heavily in the dissolution of his marriage, cost him his job and his relationship with other detectives. It would also almost take his life.

Laying down the law

Bar Jonah called Bob and told him to bring Roland to the jail to see him. Late in the afternoon toward the end of February, Bob showed up at the detention center with Roland in tow. Roland was stymied by all the rigmarole that it took to get into the jail. Bob had been through it all before with Bar Jonah; it was only a minor inconvenience for him. Bar Jonah made sure he already had tears rolling down his cheeks when he came through the door and first laid his longing eyes on Roland. He could barely contain his excitement at seeing the son he had never had. Bar Jonah gave Roland one of his famous "bear hugs" and told him how much he missed him and reminded him of the fun they had together. But, Bar Jonah explained, the cops were lying about him again. He guessed it was just his bad luck that the cops came after him for things he didn't do. It made him think that he had Indian blood or something. Roland said he understood. The cops were always coming after the Indians. Bar Jonah asked Roland if the cops had been around asking questions about him. Roland said he didn't think so. He thought one cop had come around, but Lori didn't tell him anything and sent him on his way. Bar Jonah then looked pleadingly at Roland and told him that it was *very* important that he not tell the cops anything about the fun they'd had together. Like Bar Jonah had always protected Roland, now it was Roland's turn to protect Bar Jonah, especially now that he was so vulnerable. Bar Jonah's rheumy eyes told Roland how scared he was. Roland told Bar Jonah that he shouldn't worry, he would take care of him and not tell the cops anything. Bar Jonah whispered to Roland that he was also scared that social services would take him and Stormy away from Lori because she wasn't home much. It would break Bar Jonah's heart if his boys had to go live with some white family, far away from his own people. That wouldn't be right. Bar Jonah told Roland that he would never say anything that would get him and Stormy in trouble either. It was best if they made a pact, right then and there, not to say anything to anyone about how much time they'd spent together and the fun things they did. Roland thought that was a good idea too. He wouldn't tell anyone anything. Bar Jonah told Bob to take Roland out for a big lunch after they left the jail. Roland should sure think about being a U.S. Marshal instead of a chef, Bar Jonah said. The Marshals always needed men who are as brave as Roland.

Back on track

On March 16th, 2000, Cameron officially took the reins of the case. He had been in touch with Wilson, who along with Bellusci, filled him in on the particulars. That morning Cameron arranged to meet Wilson and Detective Tim Theisen at the police department at six a.m. They went straight to the south drying room of the police gymnasium. Cameron was carrying the first of his daily dozen cups of coffee. Late in the afternoon on that snowy March day, Lieutenant Corky Groves approached Cameron in the hallway while he was getting another cup of coffee. Groves told Cameron that he wanted the case against Bar Jonah solved in a month. "He was pretending to be a fucking cop and carrying a concealed weapon," Groves said. "Get him a couple of years in lockup and help keep our numbers up." Cameron shook his head in disbelief, called Groves an idiot and walked away. Groves became incensed and screamed that he was going to have Cameron fired for insubordination. Cameron yelled back and told Groves that they could go to Chief Jones's office right then and there.

Groves had vowed to push the Ramsay case when he came back from the FBI Academy in '97. The other detectives sitting at their desks watched the spectacle unfold. One detective said he thought Cameron and Groves were going to come to blows, when Cameron accused Groves of only focusing on Rachel Howard because she was his "lazy ass way out." As Cameron turned and walked away, he muttered that Bellusci had fucked up the case from the beginning and Groves not only let him, but encouraged him. He also remembered that Bar Jonah was listed as number "40" on Bellusci's list of suspects when Zach disappeared.

* * *

Cameron, Wilson and Theisen started the arduous process of sifting through the dozens of boxes of material taken from Bar Jonah's apartment. They began sorting through Bar Jonah's scribbled writings, trying to make sense of the seemingly meaningless, random letters he had written across the blue lined pages in an orange spiral notebook. Cameron couldn't quite figure out why it was lying there, but on top of one of the boxes was a short report from the Doctors Convenience Care Clinic, that was across the street from Bar Jonah's apartment, when he lived in Bob's duplex. The report was dated February 6th, 1996. Cameron picked up the report and read that at 2:20, Bar Jonah had gone to the clinic to be treated for an injured thumb and index finger. He had also complained that his right leg hurt. Dr. Engbrecht's note said that he had prescribed Bar Jonah an anti-inflammatory and pain medication.

The quarter-inch, plywood plank that had been found in Bar Jonah's bedroom during the search was propped up against the tile wall of the gymnasium. Cameron laid the board on the buffed waxed floor, squatted down and traced his fingers around the couple of dozen, triangular shaped holes. Some of the holes were all of the way through to the other side. Standing up and looking down, from what he called an aerial view, Cameron saw that the holes in the board lined up perfectly with where the tendons would be for a child about the size of Zach. Without saying a word, Cameron left the gymnasium and drove to a lumber yard not too far from the police department. There he bought a small piece of quarter inch plywood, the same thickness as the one found in Bar Jonah's bedroom.

Wilson and Theisen wondered what Cameron was up to when he walked back into the gymnasium with the piece of plywood tucked under his arm. He was also carrying a hunting knife with a beveled tip that he had picked up at his house on the way back. Cameron laid the small piece of plywood on the floor and said to Wilson and Theisen, "Watch this." Then Cameron took the hilt of the knife in his right hand and slammed the tip of the blade into the plywood. With a resounding blow, he drove the point of the knife all the way through the wood and into the floor of the gymnasium. When the apex of the blade had slammed into the board, Cameron's hand had slipped; his thumb and forefinger were jammed so far back, that he joked that he was going to go over to the Doctors Convenience Care Clinic to see Dr. Engbrecht.

For Cameron, Wilson and Theisen, Bar Jonah became their only priority. They knew there was more to the case than Bar Jonah being out for a morning stroll, dressing up like a cop, carrying a stun gun. Cameron also knew that the impersonating a cop charge would never hold up in court. Even though Bar Jonah was dressed in all of the trimmings of a police officer, he had not attempted to approach anyone. Therefore, he could dress however he wanted.

Wilson had been involved in the Zach Ramsay case from the beginning. He was never convinced that Rachel Howard was the culprit in her son's disappearance but had been pushed to pursue her by Scott Cruz. After Zach vanished, Bellusci and Cruz had pushed hard for everyone to see it their way, even though there was not a shred of evidence, other than the elusive missing four hours. However, throughout the remainder of his career as a police officer, Bellusci would never stop focusing on Rachel Howard as the primary suspect.

Theisen too had been involved interviewing witnesses when Zach disappeared. He was appalled at how the FBI had polygraphed Rachel Howard. Theisen was the only police polygrapher in the state of Montana and knew the manner in which Rachel's polygraph was conducted by the FBI would have invalidated its results. Like Cameron, Theisen had never been convinced of the direction that Bellusci had taken the case.

Those long hours

Bar Jonah sat in his cell, waiting for another miracle to happen. His public defender was trying to prepare a case challenging the impersonating and concealed weapons charges, while hearing rumors that other charges were on the horizon. There was something wrong with the guy, Bar Jonah's public defender kept saying to himself. He couldn't shake the feeling. Bar Jonah continued to maintain his steadfast innocence. He had done nothing. However, Bar Jonah was sure a killer was out there, even though no one had said anything to him yet about being suspected of killing Zach. He told his attorney that he would be glad to help the police, if they would just ask. To occupy his time, Bar Jonah began writing more poetry. On March 19th, Bar Jonah wrote *The Tiger In Me*.

THE TIGER IN ME JUST STRIKES OUT AT ANY VICTIM HE SEES,
REGARDLESS THE GENDER, NATIONALITY, OR CREED.
SO MANY TIMES I LOCKED IT UP IN A DARK, DARK HOLE,
BUT YOU HEAR IT GROWLING DAY OR NIGHT
AND CAUSES A TOLL.
ON THE PATIENTS AND BARRIERS I BUILT UP,
TO CONTROL THE TIGER SO IT WON'T ERUPT.
AND SPRING TO ITS NEXT VICTIM,
BUT I FOUND OUT YOU CAN'T DO IT ON YOUR OWN
BECAUSE IT JUST DOESN'T DIM.
I AM THE KEEPER AND THE TIGER,
I CAN NEVER TAKE MY EYE OFF THE TIGER.
OR OFF THE GOD WHO HAD GIVEN ME THE
STRENGTH TO TAME THE BEAST,
I WAS FREED FROM THE ROAR OF REMORSE.
THE GROWL OF GUILT AND THE RAGING OF MY EVIL,
NO MORE WILL ANYONE BE IN PERIL.
FOR I'M FREE FROM THE TIGER IN ME,
BECAUSE I SEE IT NOW IN ME.

Below the poem, Bar Jonah scribbled, "*Amusement and instruction, taste and deporum were circulated among a people dominated 'A Reading Nation;'—But who ever heard of a sinner being brought to true repentance.*" A few minutes after he finished *The Tiger In Me*, Bar Jonah wrote his last will and testament:

I, Nathaneal Bar Jonah, being of sound mind and a great sense of humor request the following done on my behalf after I'm gone or incapacitated.

1. *My family will not assume any financial responsibility for any of my debts.*
2. *If I'm paralyzed and on feeding tube, those feeding tubes will be removed and you will let me die. If I'm on life support, you will pull the plug and you will let me die.*
3. *I wish to be cremated and my ashes scattered in the mountains.*

4. *At my memorial service I would like these songs played or possibly sung by Russ Michaels. They are as follows:*

- Mama Tried *by Merele Haggard (for my mom)*
- Time In A Bottle *by Jim Croce (for my family and friends)*
- These Are A Few Of My Favorite Things *(A Song from "The Sound of Music," one of my favorite movies)*
- He The Pearly Gates Will Open *(my favorite hymn)*
- Front Seat, Back Seat by Love Song *(Christian Music 1970s)*
- Through It All by Andre Crouch *(This song is the one that saved my life when I was about to commit suicide in 1977)*
- I Pledge Allegiance To The Lamb *by Ray Boltz*
- The Sun Will Come Out Tomorrow—*(Movie "Annie")*

5. *My final wish is that no one mourns for me. Instead, I want you to celebrate my death. I mean party on dude for I'm going to a place where there is no more pain or sorrow. Gee, it sure sounds like heaven to me. Oops! You know what? It is! Silly me! You know Pastor Russ, I can remember when you visited me in jail in that little booth and you said that you didn't think you could hold up as well as I did. Well, the truth is that for the 14 years I spent in prison God never left my side. I saw big miracles and small ones and I expected at least one miracle a day from God. He always came through. I witnessed a full pledged Satanist give his life over to God and a guard known for his cruelty toward prisoners and he showed compassion toward me. I had an inmate rip my Bible in half to get back at me and 3 days later in the mail I got a brand new one. I've been raped by several guards on the same bloody mattress where they had killed an inmate just hours before while they videotaped the whole thing for training purposes. So I guess you could say I made my first porn flick although an unwilling participant. I've seen the good and the bad in people. Yet through it all, God kept me safe and he has always been there for me. He never faltered in his love for me. That's quite a comfort in a time of turmoil. God cares enough about a little sparrow, so, how much more does he care about you and me. So, what do*

110

I have to worry about? I've seen God take a hopeless situation like when all avenues were closed it seemed and I'd never, ever be released. Yet God told me I would and I believed him even though the evidence of my release was not there. Then totally out of left field I got 2—yes, 2—Christian psychiatrists who believed in me. That was a miracle in itself to find 2 Christians in that profession in Massachusetts. The state had a lot of evidence on their side, yet the judge sided with me. Another miracle for sure and even when I had to stay in prison 4 additional months due to a clerical error I still believed God's promise to me even though my friends told me I was crazy. So, just keep your eyes on Jesus and he'll always be there for you no matter what. Just keep expecting that miracle. Well, with that I'll close.

Love Ya'all,
Nathan Bar Jonah

Bar Jonah then had the jail notary emboss the great seal of the State of Montana on the paper in red ink.

Putting the pieces together

While Bar Jonah was in his cell writing poetry and his will, Cameron, Wilson and Theisen were poring over thousands of pages of records from Bridgewater State Hospital. One statement contained in a psychological profile developed by psychiatric social worker, Ann Gillaspy, particularly struck the investigators. Gillaspy wrote, "Bar Jonah's sexual fantasies, bizarre in nature, outline methods of torture extending to dissection and cannibalism; he expresses a curiosity about the taste of human flesh. He also has images of electrifying beds and man-eating fish." Out of more than a dozen psychological and psychiatric evaluations, Gillaspy was the only evaluator who identified Bar Jonah as using the highly complex and primitive psychological process known as projective-identification. Ms. Gillaspy even

111

went so far as to speculate that projective-identification was the cornerstone of Bar Jonah's predatory nature. Unfortunately her discerning observations were ignored.

Right before Cameron came back from another of his many coffee sojourns, Wilson found the list of names Bar Jonah had scribbled on a piece of yellow paper, that Bellusci had found during the initial search.

ROLANDBAERNATHYSTORMYA
BERNATHYBARRYFLANNIGANE
RIKSCHMIDTLOGANIHCKSER
IKHATHAWAYNATHANORDJON
NATHANAELBENJAMIN
LEVIBARF-JONAHBJNATHA
NNATEDAVIDPAULBROWNDA
VEMICHAELLEONARDJARO
MINSKITAMMYMARIEJAROM
INSKIMANDYLEEJAROMINS
KILOISANNJAROMINSKI
FOSHAYLEEFOSHAYSHAWN
MICHAELWATKINSJULIE
WATKINSSHAWNMICHAELR
OSSINNIKKIROSSINMISSYRO
SSINZACKERYRAMSEYCHRIS
WESTPHALLMICHAELSURPRIS
EBILLYBENOITALENRICKIASDIED

As Cameron, Wilson and Theisen began to deconstruct the list, they began to see a troubling pattern emerge. Who were these people and why was the last word on the list *DIED*. When they peeled the words apart, individual names came clearly into view

Roland Baernathy
Stormy Abaernathy
Barry FlanniganErik Schmidt

Logan Hicks
Erick Hathaway
Nathan Jordan,
Nathaneal Benjamin Levi Barjonah,
BJ, Nathan, Nate, David Paul Brown, Dave
Michael Leonard Jarominski
Tammy Marie Jarominski
Mandy Lee Jarominski
Lois Ann Jarominski Foshay
Lee Foshay
Shawn Michael Watkins
Julie Watkins
Shawn Michael Rossin
Nikki Rossin
Missy Rossin
Zackery Ramsey
Chris Westphall
Michael Surprise
Billy Benoit
Al Enrickias
Died

The investigation immediately began to shift to a higher sense of priority when they discovered Zach Ramsay's name on the list.

* * *

On Monday, March 20th Cameron and Theisen believed it was necessary to talk with Rachel Howard. Rachel had moved about a hundred miles northeast of Great Falls to Choteau, Montana, a beautiful, out-of-the-way community that sits close to the far eastern edge of Glacier National Park. Before Cameron and Theisen left Choteau, they informed Rachel that she was no longer a suspect in her son's disappearance. The meeting with Rachel lasted less than two hours.

After Cameron and Theisen got back to their offices, Cameron noted on his CONTINUATION REPORT FORM, "Missing Person Cr# 96-3379 Detective Theisen and myself went to Choteau, Montana and met with Rachel Howard. We advised her that we would be working on the case. We spoke with Rachel for approximately 1.5 hours. Rachel was shown a picture of Nathan Bar Jonah. Rachel did not know him. Rachel spoke with us at length about the investigation and the accusations that she had killed her son. Rachel was consistent today, as she was four years ago. Rachel stated she did not kill her son. Rachel has faith that Zach is still alive, wherever he is. Rachel was given some information as to the direction this investigation is heading. I was up front with her and told her that at this time, I believe that a stranger took Zach. I also told her that there is a possibility that Zach has been killed. Rachel was appreciative of the up front information about the possibilities that Zach could have been killed. After the interview with Rachel, I am comfortable in saying that she is cleared as a suspect in the disappearance of her son, Zachary Ramsay." Cameron added, "Additional relatives to include the father, Franz Ramsay; Franz's wife, Cindy; and Rachel's boyfriend, Carl DeKoning, also will not be pursued at this time without further information. All of the aforementioned individuals were interviewed extensively and took polygraph examinations. Nothing surfaced at the time of the original investigation that would indicate that they were involved."

Late in the afternoon on March 22nd, Cameron and Theisen tracked down Bob. When they met with Bob they found him to be helpful. But Cameron also thought he was very clean and very odd. Bob explained that he didn't know his brother very well and until Bar Jonah moved to Great Falls in '91, he really didn't have much to do with him. However, he would always support his brother. Bob also said that his mother had dedicated her life to Bar Jonah. In Cameron's daily journal on the progress of the case he said, "Bob asked us if we had ever dragged the river for Zachary Ramsay and also asked if we checked the dump. Bob said that he was trying to think like Nathan. He thought that if Nathan was involved he would have panicked and become very angry." Bob said Tyra couldn't take it anymore and had moved back to Dudley to live with Lois and her family. They had remodeled part of their business complex into a nice apartment for Tyra. She would be close by where they could keep an eye on her in case she became ill. It took her almost two weeks but she managed to drive all the way from Great Falls to Dudley by herself. Tyra was now 82.

* * *

One of the items Bellusci had originally recovered was Bar Jonah's check registers and cancelled checks. When Cameron reviewed Bar Jonah's check register from the first part of October 1995 to February of 1996 he found that Bar Jonah took a cab on few occasions in late 1995. But Bar Jonah's use of cabs dramatically increased in February '96. Bar Jonah usually had about five to seven pages of checks that he had written listed in his registry. From October '95 until January '96 there were a few entries indicating he had taken a cab, usually Diamond Cab out of Great Falls. But in February 1996, Bar Jonah's check registry revealed only one page of activity and six of the nine entries were written to Diamond Cab. Bar Jonah's register showed that he had written checks for:

Check #3684, Deaconess Hospital, $40, dated 2/5
Check #3685, Diamond Cab, $6.75, dated 2/6
Check #3686, Diamond Cab, $6.75, dated 2/7
Check #3687, Town Pump, $4.29, dated 2/7
Check #3688, Diamond Cab, $6.50, dated 2/8
Check #3689, Diamond Cab, $6.75, dated 2/9
Check #3690, Diamond Cab, $6.75, dated 2/9
Check #3691, Diamond Cab, $5.75, dated 2/10
Check #3692, Subway, $4.88, dated 2/10

Bar Jonah's check registry abruptly ended on February 10th and didn't begin again until March 10th. Cameron didn't see this as fitting Bar Jonah's pattern of record keeping and wondered why Bar Jonah had changed his habit.

On March 22nd, Cameron received a call from Diamond Cab. They had located the radio logs from February 6th to February 10th, 1996. Cameron wanted the logs because he was trying to figure out where in the hell Bar Jonah had gone during that span of time. He wanted to compare if the checks in Bar Jonah's check registry matched Diamond Cabs radio logs.

The cab runs showed a pattern that seemed to indicate that Bar Jonah did not use his car from February 6th through February 10th. Cameron told Theisen that in searching the rest of the check registry, there was nothing to indicate that Bar Jonah had ever used a cab as often as he did around the time that Zach disappeared. Cameron wondered if Bar Jonah was using cabs to revisit the crime scene. In his review of Bar Jonah's criminal behavior, Cameron knew that Bar Jonah had also used a cab when he threatened the Surprise family after the incident at the Oxford Post Office in 1991.

The cab rides continued to make Cameron, as he called it, itch. His check registry was right there telling Cameron when Bar Jonah took a cab. But Cameron couldn't shake the sense that something within the sequence of cab rides here and there, was not adding up.

Late on the afternoon of the March 23rd, Cameron played a hunch and decided to subpoena the bank's photostat copies of Bar Jonah's cancelled checks. When the checks arrived at the police department, Cameron began scrutinizing the bank's photostats against Bar Jonah's originals. The first check Cameron examined was number 3686, dated February 6th, 1996, written to Diamond Cab. Bar Jonah had taken a cab from Hardee's to 1116 1st Avenue South. The amount was $6.75. The cab dropped Bar Jonah off a block away from his home.

The moment Cameron lay Bar Jonah's check, number 3686, beside the bank's microfilmed copy, was the moment that he knew that Bar Jonah had killed Zach Ramsay.

* * *

The date on check number 3686 had been carefully erased, changing the date from February 7th, 1996 to February 6th, 1996. It was clear that once Bar Jonah received the check back from the bank, he erased the date he had actually written on the check and made it one day earlier. Bar Jonah later said that he had no memory of changing the date, but he guessed that someone at the bank had changed it before they sent it back to him. It was beginning to look like another conspiracy had developed against him. Cameron was likely the mastermind.

Cameron also examined check number 3685. With the cab records it was established that check number 3685 was written on February 7th. The check was used for a cab ride from 1216 1st Ave. South to Hardee's. Bar Jonah wrote the date on this check as February 8th, 1996.

Bar Jonah had taken the two checks that he had written on February 7th and made it appear that he had written one on the 6th and one on the 8th. He worked on the 7th, yet he left the memo blank on these two checks. When Cameron checked all of Bar Jonah's checks from January 26th, 1996 to February 10th, 1996, he always wrote in the memo "transportation to work" or "transportation from work". On the two checks that were written on February 7th Bar Jonah left the memo blank and then altered check number 3686 to make it appear that he wrote it on February 6th. The day Zach Ramsay vanished. Bar Jonah kept the altered check, in his desk drawer, separate from all his other cancelled checks, for four years. He did not take a cab on February 6th but wanted someone to think that he had. Cameron believed that Bar Jonah was trying to set up an alibi and wanted to show that he did not use his mother's car on the day or the day after Zach disappeared. Cameron called

117

Wilson and Theisen, telling them to meet him at his office. Even with Wilson's bone-dry demeanor, he was ecstatic when Cameron went through what he had discovered. Theisen, however, threw a blanket over Cameron's and Wilson's smoldering enthusiasm with a sobering question. Okay he killed him, but what in the hell did he do with Zach's body?

* * *

In Cameron's digging he also found a receipt showing that Bar Jonah rented a silver 1990 Chevrolet Celebrity station wagon from Practical Rent-A-Car on January 29th, 1996. Bar Jonah returned the car on February 5th at 3:30. He had driven 510 miles. When he returned the car, the lot attendant jokingly asked Bar Jonah where the hell he'd been to put that many miles on the car. Bar Jonah told him to mind his own fucking business.

CHAPTER SEVEN

Anthropophagus

Cameron, Wilson and Theisen were all now convinced that Bar Jonah had killed Zach Ramsay. But they continued to struggle with where Bar Jonah had dumped the young boy's body. On the last day of March, Cameron, Wilson and Theisen were sitting in Cameron's office, with the orange spiral bound notebook flipped open on the desk. The notebook was turned sideways. Cameron was sitting with his chin cupped in his hands staring at a page of random letters written ten deep and about forty-two across.

NIQASUTSEHEDARKNIAEDEDSLOEBNXETANHLJEAAPC
MAAITRNITLOAEWNVIDITMBHYARZROIJATOSTNTLAEEHDM
DCIAHDVLDILEDDSPLSAIEUTRLTT8LREOBWONYLSUTNECW
HBARBEGELPENPRAISEGREENHANGEMHIGHHAPPYHALLOWEENC
ASRLSOSFPGOSETRESUSNSESICEETISLTLOYOPEEIEA
SAOERATDIRATDUKYOPADTWMNM APEITEBPTISPNSSR
EUMFECFIDIAASXRLEMSRBTNSCIGHLTLOYPHSNSCI
YMYRNHREKDNLEOASXAATAIGUKNTEITEBSEIADUKN
GTRFNLNTEITEOADIIGIOREAAHUKNHRNEVANFRHF
IDYODIGHLTLBYNGVNHMHRBTFCISEIHRGIADTEN

Wilson made a smart-aleck remark asking Cameron if he had it all figured out yet. Cameron looked up and told Wilson to fuck off. Then Cameron looked back down at the page. Suddenly Cameron saw sixteen letters jump out from the array and begin to pulse …

NIQASUTSEHEDARKNIAEDEDSLOEBNXETANHLJEAAPC
MAAITRNITLOAEWNVIDITMBHYARZROIJATOSTNTLAEEHDM
DCIAHDVLDILEDDSPLSAIEUTRLTT8LREOBWONYLSUTNECW
HBARBEGELPENPRAISEGREENHANGEMHIGHHAPPYHALLOWEENC
ASRLSOSFPGOSETRESUSNSESICEETIS*LTLOYOPE*EIEA
SAOERATDIRATDUKYOPADTWMNMAPE*ITEBPTIS*PNSSR
EUMFECFIDIAASXRLEMSRBTNSCIGHLTLOYPHSNSCI
YMYRNHREKDNLEOASXAATAIGUKNTEITEBSEIADUKN
GTRFNLNTEITEOADIIGIOREAAHUKNHRNEVANFRHF
IDYODIGHLTLBYNGVNHMHRBTFCISEIHRGIADTEN

Wilson later said that Cameron almost broke his eardrum when he screamed, "My God, he ate him!"

Cameron drew a curvilinear line, snaking diagonally around the letters, to show Wilson and Theisen how they spelled out the phrase *LITTLE BOY POT PIES*. Wilson took the page from the notebook and went to work, attacking it like a word puzzle. Before joining the FBI, Wilson had been an accountant. Discerning patterns was not only his specialty but also his passion. In a few minutes he found multiple sequences that spelled out,

PENISES ARE YUMMY
FRENCH FRIED KID
BARBEQUED KID AND MY LITTLE KID DESERT
LUNCH IS SERVED ON THE PATIO WITH ROASTED CHILD
LITTLE BOY STEW

When Cameron flipped the page there was another set of jumbled letters run together in the same fashion as the first,

NATHANBENJAMINLEVIBARJONAHBJNATHANN
ATEDAVIDPAULBROWNBARRYFLANNIGANVICTUALS
LITTLEBOYSTEWROASTEDTURKEYANDHAMCOOKEDO
NTHEBARBYBARBEQUESBEEESUMYUNGGUYGAYBLAD
ESAREMYFAVORITEFOODCHRISTMASDINNERFORTWO
BOYSSCHOOLGIRLSSCHOOLCHILDRENSSPORTSFAMILYANDCON
QUERTHEPLEASUREZONESEXONTHEBECHANDEVERYWHER

Now that they knew they were looking for sequences, the second bunch came apart easier than the first.

1. Nathan Benjamin Levi Bar Jonah
2. BJ
3. Nathan
4. Nate
5. David Paul Brown
6. Barry Flannigan Victuals
7. Little Boy Stew
8. Roasted Turkey and Ham
9. Cooked on the Barby Barbeques Beee Sum Yung Guy
10. Gay Blades are my favorite food
11. Christmas dinner for two
12. Boys school
13. Girls School
14. Childrens sports
15. Family and friends
16. Babysitting minors
17. Hitchhikes surprise and conquer the pleasure zone sex on the bech and everywher

* * *

121

Right before they decided to call it quits for the night, Wilson pulled out a list of names, written on a white piece of paper that was folded in half and slipped unobtrusively between the last two pages of the orange spiral bound notebook. At the top of the paper, Bar Jonah had simply written *Lake Webster*. The Lake Webster list was twenty-six names of boys and girls. On the left side of the page was a year, followed by a name and what appeared to be the age of the child. There was some type of code after several of the names, particularly the ones further down the list. The last entry on the right side of the page appeared to be a pseudonym.

Lake Webster

1963	Mary Paquette	6		=	Lori Eppard	
1964	Ray Frenier	10 BICH/E		=	Michael Cook	
1965	John Peterson	9		=	Ryan Suarez	
1966	Peter Murray	9		=	Evan Hodges	
1967	Kevin Lebrec	8		=	Zach Everton	
1966	Bobby Patterson	6		=	Brandon Myers	
1968	Brian Joy	5 ANH/R		=	Kevin Vinokur	
1968	Wayne Bellis	5		=	Andy Frakes	5½
1968	Kenny McIntyre	11		=	Wade Bramlin	
1977	Billy Benoit	13		=	John Dziak	
1969	Bobby Harris	8 BLDH/BE		=	Ben Rozela	
1977	Al Enrickais	14		=	David West	
1970	Mark Lawson	9 BLDH/E		=	Daniel Martinez	
	Ben Lawson	11 (+ Parents)		=	Eleanor Martinez	
1971	Kim Gion	11		=	Annie Marie Falor	
1971	Chad Morin	7		=	Andy Van Denend	
	Todd Morin	9		=	Peter Van Denend	
1972	David St. Lawrence	14		=	Steven Curnow	
1974	Richard O'Connor	8		=	Ahmed Shah Durrani	
1975	Bobby Donaldson	9 RLH/E		=	Michael James McClain	
1975	Brian Knapp	9 BDLH/BE		=	Steve Berman	

1975	Wesley Myers	9 BICH/E	=	Jeff Hamilton
1975	Bruce Shenkel	17 BEH/E	=	Tom Stennes
1976	B David Cooper	10 BICH/R	=	Kevin Peterson
1976	Jeffrey Jamioga	10 BKH/BE	=	Erik Gorczynski
1976	Tommy Smith	10	=	Paul Catlin
1977	John Bauman	11	=	John Mann

The question for the investigators was not only who were these children but were they still alive?

Now with the belief that Bar Jonah had eaten Zachary Ramsay, the investigation began to take on a macabre undertone. If Bar Jonah had cannibalized Zach, then his bones had to be somewhere. Bob had told Cameron and Theisen about Pam and Sherri. Cameron also found letters back and forth between Bar Jonah and Pam. The tone of the letters went from *I can't live without you* to *get out of my life*. He also found several letters between Bar Jonah and Sherri. All of those were of the *get out of my life* variety. Cameron decided that it would be necessary to interview both women.

First though, Cameron needed to get a judge to authorize a search warrant for Bob's apartment building. In meticulous detail, Cameron wrote a thirteen-page probable cause statement to Judge McKittrick, carefully outlining Bar Jonah's criminal history and witness statements.

To the Honorable Judge McKittrick,

With the information gathered so far it is imperative that we apply for search warrants for the following property used by Nathan Bar Jonah in the year 1996:

1. A complete search for forensic evidence of a 1987 Toyota Corona 4 door white, lic# 2P-9989F, Vin# JT2AE82E5H3548558 owned by Tyra Brown and Jill Brown. The car is located in Dudley, Massachusetts and is still owned by Tyra Brown. This car was the only means of transportation that Nathan Bar Jonah had in February of 1996 besides the use of a cab. If

Zach Ramsay was abducted, a car had to have been used. A light colored car of similar appearance was seen in the area at the time of the last sighting.

2. A complete search of the residence located at 1216 1 Ave. South, to include the basement which Bar Jonah had access to in February of 1996. To include the unattached 3-stall garage located to the rear of the duplex. To include the ability to take a cadaver dog through the attached duplex of 1218 1 Ave. South to try and locate any scent of Zach Ramsay. Description of duplex is as follows. A yellowish duplex with beige trim containing 1216 and 1218 1 Ave. South. A full basement containing an apartment owned by Bob Brown, Bar Jonah's brother. An unattached yellowish 3-stall garage with a dirt floor, 3 large wood doors.

3. A complete forensics kit on Nathaniel Bar Jonah to include hair and blood for comparison to any evidence that may be located during this investigation.

McKittrick didn't blink when he signed the search warrants.

Traveling east

Early in the morning on April 3rd, Cameron, Wilson and Theisen boarded a plane for Massachusetts. They got to Boston about 5:30, rented a car and drove about an hour up to Dudley. Cameron had made arrangements with the duty officer at the Sturbridge State Police Barracks, before they left Montana, to have Tyra's car transported from Dudley. Cameron and Theisen would sweep the car for evidence and fingerprints. The Massachusetts State Police had requested that Cameron bring an original copy of the search warrant.

Cameron was furious when the barracks duty officer called him late in the afternoon on the 4th. "We can't get the car down here for you," he said. "If you want it, you're

going to have to make arrangements to get it here yourself."
The call was abrupt and there was no discussion or explanation. They just couldn't do it. Cameron called Bar Jonah's brother-in-law, Lee Foshay, who generously offered to drive Tyra's Toyota to the Sturbridge Barracks the next day. When Cameron and Theisen arrived at the police barracks on the morning of the 5th, the lieutenant requested the original search warrant. Cameron pulled the folded up warrant out of his inside sports jacket pocket and handed it to the officer. The lieutenant unfolded the warrant and quickly glanced over it just as Lee Foshay was pulling into the barracks with Tyra's Toyota. The lieutenant looked up and told Cameron that he didn't believe there was sufficient probable cause to justify searching the car. The three men argued for almost two hours. The lieutenant wouldn't budge. He was steadfast that Cameron and Theisen were not going to search the car. Lee Foshay stood by and watched the spectacle. It finally reached the point that Cameron called Special Agent Jerry Downs, an FBI profiler based out of Quantico, who had been working peripherally with Wilson on developing a psychological picture of Bar Jonah. Before the end of the day, the duty officer received a Federal Search Warrant authorizing Cameron and Theisen to search Tyra's Toyota. Cameron said that he thought the authorities in Massachusetts would bend over backwards to cooperate, given how they were the ones who sent Bar Jonah to Montana. In fact, they couldn't have been more uncooperative.

That night Cameron and Theisen went out and got drunk. Cameron knew he wasn't going to sleep well. He thought somehow it might help. The nightmares and sweats had begun the night Cameron proclaimed that Bar Jonah had eaten Zach. He couldn't shake the images. Like any cop, Cameron thought he'd seen just about everything. A pedophile was bad enough but some sick fuck eating a little boy was someplace his mind had never ventured.

It was about 5:30 when Cameron and Theisen first walked into the bar. Theisen immediately struck up a conversation with a man holding a basketball. It wasn't just any ball, it was an NBA regulation game ball. Very expensive and with a dream bounce. It didn't take long before Theisen had snatched the spinning ball from the man's up-tipped index finger. Theisen was enthralled and started bouncing the ball around his body and between his legs. The man, taken with Theisen's excitement, told him to keep the basketball, he had a whole car full, he said. He traveled the country supplying the NBA with regulation game balls. Theisen continued to bounce the ball behind the hostess as she walked him and Cameron to their table. Once they sat down, Theisen rolled the ball around his neck and down his arm, dropping it perfectly into an ashtray sitting in the middle of the high, round, chrome legged table. Cameron casually swigged back a long drink of his beer and sourly said no one was applauding. Several hours and many beers later Cameron and Theisen were drunk. Very drunk. Then Theisen started telling Cameron about a suicide that he had investigated right after he got his gold detective shield. Big Mick.

Big Mick was a biker from around Great Falls and he *was* big. When a call came in about a disturbance involving Big Mick, it was understood that anyone who was available responded. It was on a rainy fall day, when a Big Mick call came over the radio. Theisen pressed the foot accelerator to the floor and headed toward the address given by dispatch. What struck Theisen as odd was that Big Mick was the one who had made the call. Big Mick never needed help from the cops, he took care of things himself. When Theisen rolled up as the detective on the scene, there were black and whites aplenty, but no one seemed to be in an uproar. In fact, Big Mick was sitting with his head in his hands, sweaty and bare-chested on the busted-up brick steps in front of his house. When Theisen walked up, he stopped and asked Big Mick what the problem was. Big Mick raised his

126

head like a man pushing up a man-hole cover. Theisen said his face was ashen. Big Mick didn't say anything, he just shook his head back and forth and waved his thick palm for Theisen to go on into the house. As Theisen walked in, one of the patrol officers stopped him and said that Big Mick's best friend found out that his girlfriend at the time was fucking another man. He came over to Big Mick's, not for solace, but to kill himself. As the cop walked out the door, he told Theisen that the body was back in the bedroom.

Theisen walked into the bedroom and there sitting on the edge of the bed was Big Mick's dead best friend. He was fat too. In fact he was so fat, that his thick, blue-black bloating mid-drift, which encircled his body like an over-inflated inner tube, made him seem almost floating. Each time a cop walked across the flimsy wavy floors, Big Mick's dead best friend's belly quivered. The only thing missing was most of his head. It seemed that Big Mick's dead best friend had jacked the slide of a sawed off Remington 870, put the barrel under his chin and pulled the trigger. Pretty much, Theisen said, there was just a gaping hole on top of his neck where his head had once been. Theisen raised his eyes, tracing the trajectory of the blood splatter as he stood in front of Big Mick's dead best friend. The spew of blood and vestiges of his head that had been launched straight into the air, now formed a lumpy red speckled pattern on the once smooth white wall. But what captured Theisen's attention was not the splatter of the blood. Instead it was the bloated, blown-off lips of Big Mick's dead best friend, perfectly intact and stuck to the ceiling. Big Mick's dead best friend's bristled mustache was still attached to the sliver of skin above his tumid upper lip. As Theisen looked up at the mustache-framed lips, he wondered what Big Mick's dead best friend was about to say, right before he pulled the trigger. After Theisen finished the tale of Big Mick, Cameron looked at him, through stupored eyes and called him a sick fuck.

* * *

Cameron and Theisen stumbled out of the restaurant and began walking toward their hotel. Theisen thought he was bouncing his basketball to the rhythm of the passing traffic. Suddenly Cameron yelled "We gotta go in here," pointing to a piano store a few doors down from the bar. Only half of the overhead fluorescent lights were on and the salesman who approached them didn't seem too happy to have a couple of drunks wander into the store, especially right before closing. Theisen slurredly asked Cameron what the hell he was doing as he pulled out a black polished piano bench and bowed to an audience that was only there in Cameron's mind. Then Cameron fanned back his imaginary tux tails and sat down at the Steinway grand. Theisen was amazed when Cameron's long thin fingers began to set the ivory keys ablaze. He didn't even know that Cameron could play. Not only was Theisen impressed, so was the salesman who told Cameron to go ahead and "play us out for the night." Cameron closed up the store with the Bach Fugue in G Minor. On the flight back to Montana, Theisen also discovered that Cameron couldn't read a note of music.

* * *

While Cameron and Theisen were doing the evidence search on Tyra's car, Wilson was beginning to track down the names on the Webster list. Some of the names were familiar, like the boys Bar Jonah had tried to kill in 1977. But others had taken longer for the FBI to discover their current whereabouts.

In mid-morning, Wilson knocked on the door of the now grown-up little girl that Bar Jonah had brutally assaulted when she was happy-go-lucky and riding her bicycle, on that early June morning in 1975. It had been just a few weeks before he graduated from high school. Bar Jonah later would say that she was his graduation present to himself. The little girl was now a mother of two daughters and married to a man who worked a lot of overtime maintaining the streets of Webster.

128

When the lady of the house opened the door, Wilson identified himself with his FBI shield and politely asked her if he could talk with her about Bar Jonah. Wilson was unprepared for the woman's response. Her soft eyes turned glassy and Wilson thought that she seemed to be staring right through him. Then her body jerked backwards and she collapsed onto the floor. Her limbs and torso became so rigid, Wilson thought she was going to snap into pieces. She was trembling, seizing up and letting go, seizing up and letting go, her eyes rolling back into her head. Trickles of white foam oozed out the corners of her mouth. Wilson bent down and kept her from slamming her head onto the polished hardwood floors. After a few minutes, her body began to quiet and her eyes rolled back down to where they could focus on Wilson. He apologized and sat on the floor taking care of her until she recovered enough to sit up against the wall. She had developed seizures after Bar Jonah attacked her. They had been mostly under control for a long time now with medication. The woman had heard that Bar Jonah had been arrested in Montana and wondered if anyone would come knocking at her door. Sure enough Wilson showed up. Bar Jonah had beaten her severely, she said. He especially beat on her real bad when she vomited in his car. She didn't mean to, but the vomit just came flying up out of her throat when Bar Jonah punched her in the face. Wilson told her that he was just making sure that all of the people that had been victims of Bar Jonah were okay. He was sorry what she had been through with Bar Jonah but he was never going to get out of prison again. Montana was not going to make the same mistake that Massachusetts had. She said she was okay. She also said she was married to a good man, one who did not scare her. One who was gentle with her. Her kids were good kids too.

After Wilson left the woman's house he drove down to Boston. He pulled up about 5:30, in front of a Cape Cod style home, in a well-to-do suburb right outside of the city. A slight, handsome, boyish looking man answered the door. When Wilson identified himself as an FBI agent, Bobby Patterson, now Dr. Robert Patterson, chief of radiological oncology at a large Boston hospital, began sobbing.

Patterson had never told anyone about Bar Jonah's sexual assault. Not even his wife. Robert composed himself and graciously invited Wilson into his home. He and his wife were having dinner when Wilson had arrived. They invited him to join them but he declined, accepting a cup of coffee instead. Robert's wife was shocked by her husband's revelations. Wilson listened. Robert told in detail what Bar Jonah had done to him on Cemetery Hill. He felt guilty that he had not said something before now. Maybe he could have helped other kids, but he just couldn't talk about it. Robert had never even told his parents. But when he watched the DuPont boys throwing peaches at Bar Jonah when he got off of the school bus, Robert took secret delight and wished he had been the one hitting Bar Jonah with the rotten fruit.

Anthropology

Barely after the sun came up, Cameron knocked on Bob's door and handed him a search warrant. He was not happy. Bob believed that he had been more than cooperative and that should have been enough. The cops now wanted to search his domain. As Bob stood holding his screen door open with the toe of his shoe, he told Cameron that that shouldn't be allowed. He had done nothing wrong; he had rights. Cameron told Bob he understood. "This must be hard on you and your family," Cameron said. Cameron needed the cooperation of Bob. He did not want to alienate him or piss him off. Even though he thought Bob had some level of culpability in the way he covered for Bar Jonah, Cameron also knew that Bob, unlike his brother, was not guilty of murder. As a consolation, Cameron offered to write a letter fully exonerating Bob and the rest of Bar Jonah's family. Later that same day, Cameron wrote,

> I am a sergeant with the Great Falls Police Department, currently investigating the case of a missing child. The name of the child is Zach Ramsay. He was 10 years old on the day he disappeared. Zach was last seen alive in Great Falls Montana on February 6, 1996 as he walked to school. 4 witnesses walking down an alley saw Zach. Zach never arrived at school. A white 4-door car was seen in the area when Zach disappeared. Our investigation has now focused on Nathaniel Bar Jonah. I have been in contact with all members of Bar Jonah's family. Neither Lois, Lee, Tyra or Bob or other family members are under investigation or suspected of obstructing or tampering in any way. The family has been fully cooperative and this officer appreciates everything they have done. I have no intentions of pursuing charges against any of Nathan Bar Jonah's family or relatives.
>
> Respectfully,
> *Sgt. John Cameron*

However the letter was not enough for Bob. After he read the letter from Cameron, Bob wrote a letter complaining to Judge McKittrick.

> Dear Judge McKittrick,
>   I am writing in regards to search warrant 00-023, issued by you on 11 April 2000, for the search of my property at 1216 and 1218 1st Avenue South, Great Falls. This is of the essence and I appreciate you reading this letter. Detective John Cameron has informed me that this search is to begin on Tuesday, 18 April 2000. I believe that part of this search violates my fourth amendment rights as well as that of my tenant(s). I believe that probable cause

has not been shown for the search of the entire property and that the police/FBI have not been properly limited. Additionally I am informed that Detective Cameron will descend upon my property tomorrow with 13 police/FBI and other personnel, turning my property into a "three ring circus" and inviting unwanted news coverage. I fear that not enough consideration has been given to protecting the innocent parties in this search. I offer the following information to support my cause.

Nathaniel Bar Jonah lived at the 1216 West side of my property. He did not have access to 1218 (east side duplex). Neither did he have access to the middle of the three garages. The U.S. Constitution, supported by decisions of the Supreme Court, has placed limits on the invasion of privacy by specification. This search warrant is so broad it can be construed as non-specific. The 1218 side, its basement and middle garage should be excluded from the search warrant.

Detective Cameron has informed me that he plans to excavate two raised-log gardens in the back yard of my property. The search warrant specifically does not authorize him to do that (only the buildings are mentioned in the search warrant). Once again a search warrant must be specific. Additionally, the east side garden did not even exist in February 1996 (it was installed November 1996). Other factors, relating to common sense, come to mind as well. I check my property regularly and there were no unusual marks on the grounds at that time. Also, there are five families living on the east side of my property and three families living on the west side (surely in such a dense population someone would have seen any suspicious activity and they did not). Finally, and probably most important, the ground was frozen in February and impossible to dig. The backyard and gardens should not be excavated.

I believe that the search warrant should be restricted to the following:

1. The south bedroom of 1216 (Nathaniel Bar Jonah's bedroom in 1996).
2. The basement under 1216 only (dog search only, which is what Detective Cameron promised). The basement is currently my basement apartment home (this apartment 1218-2 did not exist until 1999). My personal property should be excluded from the search.
3. The east garage and west garage only (exclude the middle garage).
4. The police/FBI and their personnel should be restricted to a maximum of three plain-clothed personnel on my property at one time to minimize calling attention to the investigation. My good name, ability to rent in the future and even my safety are jeopardized by the "circus like" search involving 13 personnel and their vehicles which is planned for 18 April 2000. This search should be conducted as low key as possible (i.e., in plain jean clothes, no vehicles in the alley, closed garage door, etc).
5. Have the police move my personal property (currently in the east garage) to the middle garage (which should not be searched). Their plan is to move my property to a Ryder van parked in the alley (another attention getter).

In summary I will say that I have cooperated with Detective Cameron in every way possible. I have voluntarily spent over 6 hours at the police station speaking with Detective Cameron, identifying photographs and looking at evidence. I have voluntarily allowed Detective Cameron to walk through my home and garages prior to executing his search warrant. I have cooperated in every way possible, despite his embellishment of my statement in his affidavit for a search warrant, and despite unprofessional comments that have had me on an emotional roller coaster. My desire, like his, is to get to the truth. Detective Cameron believes that I have been truthful and he has signed a letter exonerating my family and me. According to Detective Cameron, the FBI profilers have stated that the likely places to check for evidence are the garage, bedroom and car (the car has already been searched). Right now it appears that he wants to kill a fly with a shotgun and it is very disconcerting to me! I respectfully ask you to please reconsider this search warrant and add the above restrictions to protect my rights. Time is of the essence! I don't want my rights trampled on and I don't want to be placed in a media circus (it jeopardizes my business, safety and good name). I would be glad to speak with you personally if you so desire.

Most sincerely,
Robert Brown

Judge McKittrick thought that parts of Bob's request were reasonable and limited the search to only areas that Bar Jonah would have had access to.

* * *

On April 12th, while Bob was preparing his letter to Judge McKittrick, Cameron was preparing to take a statement from Sherri Diederich. From reading the letters that had passed between Bar Jonah and Sherri, Cameron found out that Sherri had moved to Moscow, Idaho. Through the police in Moscow, it was easy enough to track her down. Sherri was more than willing to make a statement about the time she lived with Bar Jonah and Pam. In her statement Sherri made a litany of complaints about her ex-husband, being harassed by "certain sheriff's deputies," a referral to the Rescue Mission and the "ten dollars in horrible clothing" (which she passed on) from the Salvation Army. She also had taken away a bed and some paintings that she thought she could get about $1000 for.

When she got to Great Falls, Sherri was worried that someone was going to steal her belongings from the big yellow truck that she had packed her life into. Sherri had pawned her least treasured possessions and was continuing to hit up the Salvation Army for food and the Rescue Mission for a quick, down on your back nap. One of the pawnshops had told her about the Antique Mall. Maybe they could help her out there with her bed and paintings. Sherri told Cameron that was where she met Bar Jonah. In her statement, she detailed her relationship with Bar Jonah, saying that he was an excellent listener. The first night she was at Bar Jonah's, he told her about being raped and beaten as a boy. Sherri said they both cried when Bar Jonah told her of his horrendous childhood. She had suffered at the hands of abusers too.

The day Sherri met Bar Jonah, the owner of the Antique Mall let her put her bed and paintings on consignment in one his booths. A couple of weeks after she moved in with Bar Jonah Sherri went back to see if her bedroom set or any of her paintings had sold. The owner of the mall took her aside and said that he had heard that she was living with Bar Jonah. "Don't you know?" he asked. Sherri had looked inquisitively at the mall owner. Bar Jonah spent years in prison for raping a kid and some boy disappeared here in Great Falls a while back. Bar Jonah was a suspect then but they were never able to pin it on him. "You should be real careful around him," the owner said. Sherri went down to the courthouse and dug out the files on the Shawn Watkins case. She also said that Bar Jonah knew about a case where a little girl had been missing and someone found her bicycle. Then they brought the dogs in and finally found the child's body. Then Sherri told Cameron about the policeman and the old man.

The dig

There was still a Montana chill in the air on the morning of the April 18th, when the cavalcade of police vehicles and unmarked cars descended on Bob Brown's modest duplex on 1st Avenue South. Some parked out front, but most parked in the alley. Patrol officers, Cameron, Theisen, Wilson and a dig team from the University of Montana, Department of Anthropology set up their perimeter. They were looking for anything that might tie Bar Jonah to Zach Ramsay.

One of the uniformed officers ascended from a clapboard storm cellar, glumly shaking his head. He had not found anything. After a search of the basement apartment, Cameron decided that the main focus of the search should turn to the garage where Bar Jonah held his puppet shows. A team of graduate archeology students set up a 4 x 6 foot plastic orange tub with a 3 x 5 foot timber frame that held a wire mesh sieve. Each bucket of dirt that was hauled out of the garage was carefully poured onto the sieve. The students, all with tanned forearms from a recent trip to the Yucatan, rolled dirt from the garage floor gently through their fingers, causing it to crumble and fall through the mesh and into the orange tub. All that remained on top of the mesh was a silver charm bracelet that glistened in the bright afternoon sun, after being covered up for so many years under damp earth in a dank garage. They also found a dancing clown charm to go with the bracelet, a couple of broken black buttons, two cat-eye marbles, one blue and one green, a chipped pinkish porcelain figurine and twenty-one human bone fragments.

Cameron, Theisen and Wilson were transfixed when the bones began to show up. First, there were small, almost chip-like fragments and then the larger ones began to appear. Finally, part of what appeared to be the long bone of an arm was found buried in six inches of dirt in the middle of the garage. This was right where Mr. Popcorn Head used to sit on a wobbly white fold-up table, after the kids had gone home and the lights were turned out for the night. There was also a piece of Bar Jonah's stationery buried underneath the arm bone.

Dozens of boxes of dirt and chunks of cement were hauled from Bob's garage, back to the police department gymnasium. Theisen volunteered to go through the debris by hand to see what he might turn up. Cameron and Wilson said they would help too. For three weeks, Theisen worked day and night chipping away at the blocks of cement with a piton hammer and sifting through the piles of dirt with a wire mesh colander. He became obsessed with the concrete and the dirt. Theisen would spend hours painstakingly tapping the smoothed off rounded knuckles of concrete hoping to find more bones. After working several hours straight in what became known around the police station as the "pit", Theisen's eyes would begin to play tricks on him. He would imagine that something protruding from a chunk of concrete was a finger bone. Once Theisen was sure he found a jawbone. He would take hold of the chunks of man-made rock with his left hand and gently tap, tap, tap the area with the platypus-like end of the hammer.

On Theisen's first day as a police officer many years before, he came back into the station after being out on patrol. When he arrived, a couple of other cops were trying to subdue a suspect they had just arrested. Theisen jumped out of the cruiser to offer assistance. He quickly got into the huddle when he felt his nose break and blood go flying everywhere. Now many years later, Theisen's nose was a crooked mess. With each soft pat of the hammer, the tiny plumes of concrete dust would fly up and fill the narrow passages of his nostrils. By the end of the day, Theisen's painful, wheezing, cauliflowered nose made him look like he was the town drunk. Sometimes Cameron and Wilson would come to see how Theisen was progressing … had he found anything?, they inquired. They would even pick up a clod of dirt or two and sift it through their fingers, but Theisen bore the brunt of the task, going home each night with hundreds of tiny cuts on his hands, from the sharp edges of the rocks. Wearing gloves was not an option. Theisen thought they might interfere with him being able to feel something. Something he could otherwise miss. He was determined to chip apart every hunk of concrete and to roll each speck of dirt through his fingers. If there was something hidden, he was hell bent that he was going to find it. Theisen's hands were getting increasingly cracked and swollen the more obsessed he became with finding a bone fragment lurking in the ruins. On the last day of the second week, the pager clipped to Theisen's belt began to beep. When he reached down to press the OFF button, his index finger was so bloated that he couldn't put enough pressure on the button to turn off the alert. Frustrated, he took the handle of the chip hammer and rapped it against the top of the pager, happening to hit the OFF button, stopping the incessant intermittent tone. Theisen saw through the thin glass window that his best friend wanted him to call him. His friend had typed "911" after he entered his phone number. Theisen walked to a phone that was hanging on the wall and dialed his friend's number. He was choked up when he answered. His father had died suddenly. A heart attack. Theisen said he would be right there. His hands were so swollen that he couldn't wrap them around the steering wheel, having to steer instead with the palms.

Theisen didn't get back until about six that night. When he walked in the door of the gymnasium, Lieutenant Jere Carpenter was pacing back and forth across the buffed hardwood floor. Theisen cordially asked him why he was there so late. Carpenter in turn wanted to know why in the fuck Theisen had abandoned his post. He was supposed to be digging through the fucking dirt. Why had he stopped? Theisen looked at Carpenter, shook his head and, at that moment decided to retire the second he had his twenty.

* * *

138

Finding the bones spurred Cameron to dig deeper into Bob's property. Again Bob was disgruntled with what Cameron was proposing. He wanted to rip up Bob's yard. Tear the place apart, Bob said. Cameron and Bob went around and around. There was nothing that Cameron could find. He could dig all he wanted and there was nothing there. Bob said he was sure, because in the early summer of 1996 a "leak" had developed somewhere in the plumbing. The house was old. Bob decided to have every pipe in the place, including the entire sewer line, dug down eighteen feet, all the way to the street, torn out and replaced. Bob said that Liggett Construction did the work. As a matter of fact the trench stayed open almost the entire summer. The construction crews were given specific instructions to make sure they dug as deep as possible and to haul the old dirt away and bring in fresh new dirt to refill the trench. Bob thought it would be a good idea to give the ground a fresh start. The concrete in the basement area also had to be jackhammered out in order to get to the sewer line under the house. Bob had thought that it would be good, since he was having the plumbing done anyway, to have the place painted too. So he hired a painting crew and had them put a few coats of paint on the walls, strip the floors and replace the carpet. The place looked wonderful and smelled even better.

Cameron was dumbstruck when Bob told him about the "upgrades" he had made to the place. Finally, after a lot of haggling, Bob acquiesced and agreed for Cameron to use ground-penetrating radar to conduct a second search of his property. Cameron contacted Glacier Engineering and had them bring in the GPR they typically used on construction sites to look for any underground obstructions. It would pick up the outline of human remains also. The crew of three men stayed five hours scouring each inch of the backyard of Bob's house. But because of the soil conditions and ground moisture, the radar could only penetrate about six inches into the ground. The radar didn't show any disturbance over the area of the

139

garage where the bones had been found just a few days earlier. Cameron's captain didn't think it was worth another $1350 to bring the crew back another day, when the area would be dryer and the radar would be able to penetrate deeper into the soil. Bob agreed. After all, he had tried to tell them all along, there was nothing to be found. They just wasted a lot of money and time.

CHAPTER EIGHT

"Let us have joy in our trouble"

As the cops were digging up Bob's yard, Bar Jonah sat in jail writing letters and reading his well-worn Bible. It was the Bible that was with him while he was in Bridgewater. The Bible that had been replaced after another inmate took Bar Jonah's Book of the Lord and shredded it in front of his face, calling him a baby fucker while the other inmates laughed hysterically. But within twenty-four hours and without Bar Jonah asking anyone, a new Bible arrived unexpectedly in the mail. It was yet another miracle, he reminisced. More proof that God never wanted Bar Jonah to be far away from His Word. The guards at the Detention Center were continually surprised at Bar Jonah's contentedness and arrogance in his assuredness that he would be divinely set free. Around his mouth and chin, Bar Jonah seemed, even without many teeth, soft and even disarmingly delicate when he smiled. Much like a child sitting for the first time in front of a traveling department store photographer, wanting to put his best face forward. Perhaps it was Bar Jonah's piercing dimple, which lessened his overwhelming sense of hardness that was produced by his square brow and unflinchingly cold, aloof eyes. Bar Jonah knew that he was prone to do ill-natured things, he would sometimes admit. But nothing too bad. Nothing he couldn't be forgiven for. Nothing that he wasn't doing in the service of the Lord. Nothing that would stop him from being rescued from his enemies.

Bar Jonah would read aloud to his captors God's promise to deliver Jeremiah from his tormentors: *"I will rescue you on that day, declares the Lord; you will not be handed over to those you fear. I will save you; you will not fall by the sword but will escape with your life, because you trust in me, declares the Lord"* (KJV, Jeremiah 39:17–18). Bar Jonah considered his guards witless and prayed for them when they disrespected him by demanding that he do manual labor. He needed time to write letters, not to be mopping floors. Bar Jonah also had to begin planning his defense; his attorney was doing nothing but sitting on his ass. The guards had no idea how many things he had to take care of during the day. Bar Jonah also became quietly incensed when the guards failed to come immediately, after he told them he had a stack of letters that needed to be mailed. They were important. They needed to go out that day. Bar Jonah walked around the jail chanting Psalm 151, which God had slipped into his mind while he slept just the night before:

> *Jesus got a hold of my life and he won't let me go.*
> *Jesus got into my heart and in to my soul*
> *I used to feel oh so sad, but now I'm just so free and glad*
> *'Cause Jesus got a hold of my life and he won't let me go.*
> *1, 2, 3, The Devil's after me*
> *4, 5, 6, He's always throwing bricks*
> *7, 8, 9, He misses every time*
> *Oh, glory, hallelujah, amen!*
> *9, 8, 7, I'm on my way to heaven*
> *6, 5, 4, I'm almost at the door*
> *3, 2, 1, The devil's on the run*
> *Oh glory, hallelujah, amen!*

The guards regularly mocked Bar Jonah like the governor's soldiers mocked Jesus when they took him into the Praetorium, before they led him away to be crucified. But like Jesus, Bar Jonah forgave them. Like little children, the guards needed to be brought along. He knew they needed to begin to think more like him.

Bar Jonah could not stop collecting. For him, it was what wove together the very fabric of what he knew himself to be. In barely the blink of an eye he took everything in that was necessary to tenderize a mark to make it more supple as his prey. As soon as his eyes were set on another, he began to sop up those nearly imperceptible tokens of deeply private self-revelations that he would stroll away with from the encounter. Usually the other didn't realize that they had just lost something or how their inner life had been altered.

Bar Jonah remembered all the faces he had ever seen. He might not remember the name, but that was of little consequence. The face was what was important. Especially the eyes. Getting inside was the most important thing. Like a jewel thief, finding the right combination to the safe was what opened the door. Once inside, you just had to act like you belonged there. Not causing a ruckus, but smiling, nodding to those inner parts of another, that for a moment showed panic with the recognition that a psychic intruder has slipped in through an open eyelid. Captured, they were nestled away in his imagination, like cups hanging in a country cupboard, waiting to be filled. Bar Jonah especially sought out those with childish, anxious eyes. Those with a hunger, a longing, a pleading to be, not lured, but consumed.

* * *

The bones that were pulled out of Bob's garage were fragments. Signs of sawing or cutting were clearly defined on both edges of one of the bones. Some of them seemed to have a purplish cast to them. Cameron contacted Mitotyping

143

Technologies in Pennsylvania to see if they could extract any DNA from the sample and if they could, to see if there was a match with Zach Ramsay. They would also need a DNA sample from Rachel Howard to run the DNA against. Cameron drove up to Choteau to get a blood sample from Rachel. Even though they had found bones in Bar Jonah's garage, it couldn't be Zachary she said. Franz had had him kidnapped. He was still alive and would be home any day. She was sure of it. She and the Ladies were still working the case and keeping a close eye on Joan Cook. Rachel now had amassed even more evidence against Cook and Franz. But she wasn't ready to go to the police, especially if they were involved in the cover-up. She did agree to run over to the Teton Medical Center to get her blood drawn. Once Cameron got the blood, he drove back to Great Falls and sent out the samples late that afternoon. He enclosed the following letter to Dr. Terry Melton, Director of Mitotyping Technologies.

May 4, 2000
Att: Terry Melton, Ph.D.
1981 Pine Hall Drive
State College, PA 16801

To Whom It May Concern:

To give you a brief rundown of our case: In 1996, a 10 year old boy named Zach Ramsay disappeared while walking to school. Zach was a 90 pound, 4ft 8in, male whose mother was white and father was black. We developed a suspect named Nathan Bar Jonah. He is a 44 year old male who has spent most of his adult life in prison for attempted homicide of two 10 year old boys. We served a search warrant on a garage that Nathan Bar Jonah had used as a flea market. The flea market appeared to be a ruse to lure children into his garage. We believe that Zach was killed in the garage and possibly dismembered in the

144

garage. We had the Anthropology Department from the University of Montana excavate the garage. The garage had a dirt floor. The bone fragments we are sending you were located in the rear of the garage in the same area where a cadaver dog indicated a scent. The bones were covered with 2 inches of dirt and the garage was dark and damp. No sunlight would have penetrated the area where the bones were found.

I have sent you a blood sample from Zach Ramsay's biological mother, Rachel Howard. She is diabetic. I appreciate anything you can do to help us out on this case. Mr. Bar Jonah is currently in jail on other charges. Bar Jonah has trial scheduled for June of this year.

Respectfully
Sgt. John Cameron

* * *

During Cameron's first interview with Bob, he learned that Bar Jonah had been engaged. The woman was named Pam, Bob said. He wasn't sure when they broke up. Bob made it clear he didn't think much of her though; he thought she was crazy. Pam was one of the names on the letters that Cameron found in Bar Jonah's belongings. It took Wilson almost two weeks to track down Pam. Finally he found out she was living in Virginia Beach. Since Cameron was considered the most mild-mannered of the bunch, he was elected to call Pam. "Try to smooth talk her," Theisen whispered as her phone rang. As soon as Pam answered the phone, Cameron mouthed back to Theisen that she *was* crazy. Cameron explained that Bar Jonah was being investigated for murdering Zach Ramsay. He wanted to come to Virginia Beach and meet with Pam. Pam reluctantly agreed to meet with Cameron but said she didn't know nothin', so don't go expectin' her to be able to tell him awful much. Cameron scheduled a meeting for the second week of May.

Cameron and Wilson talked nonstop about Bar Jonah on the flight to Virginia Beach. Both men were consumed with the case. Cameron's wife was beginning to complain about the hours he was spending at the office. It was like he didn't have any set hours, she would gripe. She just didn't understand, he would counter. She complained that all she did was understand, especially about the nightmares and night sweats. Cameron was soaking the bed every night. It was hard for her to get a dry night's sleep when he was home. It would be over soon; give him just a little more time to get the case nailed down.

Wilson was obsessed too; he just kept more of it inside. His vice was eating. Wilson was a handsome man in good shape, but the Bar Jonah case was making him eat. He especially liked to drown his food in salt. It didn't help his blood pressure or the fact that he was beginning to retain water. Wilson usually got quiet and withdrew when something bothered him. He was a man who was convinced that logic and rationality governed everything. This case could be sorted out rationally.

Cameron's hand paused in mid knock just before his knuckles rapped on Pam's door. He looked at Wilson and rhetorically asked what the odd smell was that seemed to be coming under Pam's door. Wilson wrinkled his nose, sniffed, shook his head and shrugged his shoulders.

Pam set down the box of matches she was using to light candles when she heard the knock. Cameron and Wilson looked at each other and raised their eyebrows in unison, when they heard a voice behind the door say that it didn't "know nothin' about Bar Jonah." The voice yelled that it hadn't talked to Bar Jonah for a long time. Cameron knocked again identifying himself to the voice behind the door.

When the door opened, Cameron and Wilson saw a dowdy, middle-aged black woman, dressed in a frumpy, shiny

146

velveteen navy sweat suit. She had empty, dark eyes, set back in hollow, deep sockets. Her hair was more matted to the side of her head than combed. Pam's body seemed to quiver under her sweat suit, making the shimmering folds in the velveteen ebb and flow to the cadence of her palsy. Smoke from the orange tips of hundreds of trembling candles, set about her apartment, wafted around Pam like a breathing witch's cloak. Cameron thought she looked schizophrenic.

It wasn't apparent to Wilson if Pam was holding up the door jamb or if the door jamb was holding up Pam, as she rattled on and on about not knowing anything about Bar Jonah. She hadn't talked to him in a long time, she said. Cameron asked Pam if they could come inside and talk, saying that he and Wilson had come all the way from Montana to meet with her.

Pam, glassy eyed, looking right through Cameron, whimpered as she pushed herself off of the door frame with her shoulder, turned mechanically and walked back into the apartment. The cloak of smoke seemed to follow her like a whirling dervish. Aside from the smoke and the smell, Cameron and Wilson noticed the wax-caked altar nestled against a dark wall as they walked into Pam's living room. Cameron walked over to the altar, bent down, squinted his eyes and traced the thin braided dark red fissures, etched in the opaque wax, with his right index finger. Pam chuckled and told Cameron not to touch anything. The altar was sacred, Pam said. Looking up, Cameron saw dozens of dried chicken legs lined up side by side on a mahogany shelf above the altar. Lying on the floor, in the corner was what looked like a couple of flat, contorted, dried out cats, with their front paws missing. Pam tossed her arm to one side, motioning for Cameron and Wilson to sit down on a tattered and balding, purple-quilted Greek motif settee. Cameron ran his hand across the bristly thinning fabric and silently tried to recall when he still had hair. Wilson sat with his damp palms flat out on his thighs. Pam sat down in a rickety, cat-scratched varnished chair. The

147

velveteen made a soft rustle when she crossed her ample thighs. One thigh continually bounced up and down, making her foot seem to be perpetually kicking rather than rocking. Pam folded her hands and told Cameron again that she didn't know nothin' about what Bar Jonah had done. Cameron told Pam that she was not in any trouble. Pam replied she knew that she wasn't in no trouble because she hadn't done nothin' to be in trouble for.

Cameron had found some of their love letters and Bob had told him that she and Bar Jonah had been engaged. Pam said, that even though she hadn't talked to him in a long time, she still wasn't over Bar Jonah. He had been the love of her life. Then Pam said she didn't know anything about the policeman or anything like that either. Sherri was the one that knew about the policeman. Sherri had been the one who had gone through Bar Jonah's bedroom and found all those clothes and things. Wilson asked Pam if it would be okay if they just started from the beginning of her and Bar Jonah's relationship. He gently told her to tell them how she and Bar Jonah met and how they fell in love.

She then seemed to become more relaxed and told Wilson and Cameron that she was an iyalorisha of the Santería. Santería Pam said she knew she was in love with Bar Jonah the moment she discovered how much he knew about the Santería. Their meeting was meant to be. That day was blessed, as they stood together over the deep fryer breading chicken. She was ready to marry Bar Jonah by the time they got off work that day; but he didn't ask. It took a long time for Bar Jonah to realize that he needed her as much as she needed him. He was the only man she'd ever known who knew how important offering up a live sacrifice was for salvation. Pam, with bold bulging eyes, looked at Cameron and said that voodoo was irrelevant when it came down to Jesus Christ and His Blood. Bar Jonah had known about the Blood of the Lord. Pam quietly bowed her head, secretly pitying Cameron and Wilson for not understanding the Blood of Christ. When she raised her head, Pam saw Cameron nodding. Her momentary state of dejection suddenly spiraled into a state of ecstasy, when she realized that Cameron did understand the Blood. Everything in the room came alive for Pam all at once. Each flame of each candle began to rise as though it were a torch. A torch light for Christ and His Blood. Pam looked into Cameron's merciful eyes and tried to speak, but her lips were disobedient and her words could take no voice. All that had been revealed to Pam made her vulnerable eyes well up with tears. She felt like a little child. Through His Blood, the cries of the animals in the night were not cries of pain, but cries of deliverance. Pam was always willing to sacrifice herself for the Blood. The old woman, who had lived deep in the bayou and took her in when she was abandoned, taught Pam that being able to see what no one else saw and hear what no one else heard, was a special gift. "Any time you make a sacrifice for the Blood you cut away a part of yourself until one day the Blood calls you home," Pam said. The Blood is all there is, there is no more and there never will be. She could not explain it anymore to them; you either know or you don't know. Bar Jonah had known. Now Pam knew that Cameron knew. But when Pam looked into Wilson's eyes, she still felt great pity. She thought he was a pretty boy.

Pam cried as she talked about the love she and Bar Jonah shared and the pain of Bar Jonah finally breaking up and saying he didn't want to marry her. She also said that Bar Jonah insisted that sex outside of marriage was a sin and that he would have no part of it. Pam told of the conversation she had with Sherri on the first night that Sherri came between her and Bar Jonah. She thought that Bar Jonah would have married her but Sherri made a wedge between them that they couldn't take away. It may have been black magic; she wasn't sure. Pam told about Sherri showing her the sandy, dirty clothes, the bloody gardening gloves, the board in Bar Jonah's closet and a kid's coat. Sherri had said Bar Jonah pretty much admitted he'd killed the boy, chopped him up and scattered him all over the forest.

Pam began making a wheezing sound like a sheep bleating. She cocked her head back, sucked air through her nose with a loud snort, wiped her philtrum with the pad of her finger and stopped crying, saying she was sorry. Pam said she'd been praying for the missing little boy every day since she left Montana. It was a true shame he'd gone and disappeared. She just didn't know if Bar Jonah could have done such a thing. Everything she saw him do while they were together was in the service of the Lord. She had trouble figuring out his reasons for things a lot of the time but when he explained them to her, they always made sense. Maybe this was one of those times. Had Cameron and Wilson talked to Bar Jonah about this? Pam thought it'd be a real good idea if they did. He could probably clear up a lot of the questions they had. "One thing for sure," Pam said, "Bar Jonah wasn't no liar. He'd tell you right the way it was."

Pam said she'd guessed that Bar Jonah had told Sherri about being molested by a bunch of older boys when he was a boy himself. How else would Sherri know about it, Pam wondered. But Sherri had been a psychologist besides being a witch, so she probably knew how to manipulate Bar Jonah into saying things he wouldn't regularly have said. Cameron interrupted and changed the subject, asking Pam if Bar Jonah had many knives. She said he had lots of knives; she wasn't allowed to use but just a few of them. He probably had so many because he used to cut up animals and you need good sharp ones when you do that.

Pam did think it was pretty strange that Bar Jonah liked little boys so much. He loved them "more than their mommas did." He was more patient with them than he was with her. That was for sure. The garage was a kids' paradise, with all those toys and that big eye painted on the wall, Pam said. He'd lock himself in there for days on end. Wouldn't come out. It bothered her the most when he wouldn't talk to her. Around the time that boy disappeared, Bar Jonah just wouldn't have nothin' to do with Pam. When he locked himself away, Pam didn't know if he even went to the toilet. He may have just kept it all inside.

Pam snickered when she said that Bar Jonah sure got the neighbors mad at him, with all the kids hanging around back there in the alley. But he said he didn't care and told one of them off real good. The man even said he was going to hit Bar Jonah with a crooked stick. He said he didn't care; Bar Jonah didn't back down from no man. Pam said that man sure sounded like a tough guy but he sure never bothered Bar Jonah again. She even saw him popping off in the paper when that kid disappeared. He was gonna do this and he was gonna do that. Fool wasn't gonna do nothin'. Pam said she remembered seeing the search dogs and the cops walking around the neighborhood but she didn't think too much about it. But, she said, thinking back about it, she wondered why Bar Jonah's brother and his wife kept asking her where Bar Jonah was the day that boy disappeared.

Sherri had acted all nice and friendly, Pam said, but she really wanted Bar Jonah for herself. Pam had been born an iyalorisha but she sure wasn't involved in no witchcraft like Sherri was. "Sherri was a witch sure as anything," Pam said. She even knew how to read Tarot cards. Those are the cards of the witches. Pam wanted her to predict if Bar Jonah was going to marry her. But Bar Jonah had got real mad one night and threw Sherri's cards out the door and all over the yard. He wouldn't put up with any Devil worship in his house. It was a good thing though because he made Pam see that it was going against the Blood. It wasn't good to go against the Blood, no matter what. Pam told Cameron and Wilson about a time when Bar Jonah took her to a Catholic church. She had never been to any kind of church but Baptist. Bar Jonah told Pam that he thought it would be good for her to know how the Catholics

151

pretend to worship the Holy Spirit. Pam said that Bar Jonah could talk right to God; she had seen him. God answered him back too. When Bar Jonah saw someone like a Catholic profess their faith, he thought they were ridiculous, even vexing sometimes. More than anything, they were pathetic.

Bar Jonah couldn't just quote the Bible, he could recite every book of the Bible, word for word. Sometimes Pam said she got all nervous when he'd sit down and start reading to her from the Good Book, close its covers and then just go on, never missing a single word. That wasn't anything she'd ever seen anyone do before. It wasn't even like he was reading, but more like God was putting His words in Bar Jonah's mouth and he was just saying God's words right back out loud.

When Bar Jonah and Pam went to the Catholic church, he leaned over and said, not even whispering, for Pam to watch how the Catholics "put their rituals above redemption." They were just puppets with the "white-necked father" pulling their strings. There was only one Father, Bar Jonah instructed Pam. Bar Jonah sat back in the pew that day, rested his folded arms on his big belly and said to Pam that the parishioners looked like a bunch of posed waxed dolls. When everyone stood to recite the Apostles' Creed, Bar Jonah said he'd had enough of the blasphemy. He noisily raised himself from his seat and was careful to bump into a family of straw people, who had been sitting beside him and Pam. As he walked down the aisle, Bar Jonah swung his arms and tossed his hips from side-to-side, singing *We Shall Overcome*. Pam said she proudly walked right behind him, laughing so hard she thought she was going to wet her pants. Bar Jonah could be real testy when it involved lovin' the Lord. He sure wouldn't put up with *no* tomfoolery about the Lord. There was no mistakin' that. Pam said that even though she got real jealous of Sherri, in the end it was best. She'd always love Bar Jonah; she just couldn't help that. When you love someone, it's for ever and ever. You can't just stop loving someone because you know it's the best thing.

The longer Sherri stayed at Bar Jonah's, the more she snooped around and the more she found that he'd hidden here and there. Pam wished Sherri would have minded her own business. But whenever she found something she thought was funny or strange, the first thing she'd do was come to Pam and tell her about it or want to show it to her. Pam didn't want to be bothered most of the time. She really just wanted Sherri to go away. When Sherri found Bar Jonah's wigs, mascara, lipstick and lingerie, Pam said she'd had enough and told her she didn't want to know any more. But it ate at her for sure. Sometimes after Sherri showed Pam Bar Jonah's women's clothes and makeup, Pam took off her shoes and snuck real quiet down the hallway to Bar Jonah's door. One night when she did some sneaking, Pam hadn't seen the light on underneath the bedroom door. She turned the doorknob and pushed Bar Jonah's door open just a bit so she could see in. There she saw Bar Jonah by the moonlight, dressed in a short white nightie, wearing a curly blonde wig. He was just standing all frozen, staring out the window. She pulled the door closed and crept back down the hallway, put her shoes on and went out for a long walk. It was cold but that was okay, she needed to think about what she was going to do. A few days later, Sherri told her she thought that Bar Jonah was going to kill them both and they had better get away while they could if they didn't want to end up murdered and cut up like that kid.

Cameron and Wilson thought they had got all they could on that visit. Pam said they could talk to her some more if they wanted to. But she didn't want to go to court or anything and she knew that they really couldn't make her. Especially now that she lived in Virginia. Cameron assured Pam that he only wanted her help. He didn't want to cause her any problems but if she could see her way to keep helping them, they would sure appreciate it.

Cameron and Wilson were quiet at dinner that night. They knew that Pam had more information about Bar Jonah, but they also knew there was no way they or Pam could get to it. Cameron and Wilson knew there were secrets about Bar Jonah buried in the basement of Pam's broken and bewildered mind. However, Pam was not only crazy she was also fragile. To take her apart in an aggressive interrogation would be akin to psychological dismemberment. Cameron had asked Pam if he could tape their talk. She had agreed. Not only was what Pam said important, but it might also be useful to play, at least part of the tape, to Sherri and pit them against each other.

Cameron's and Wilson's plane came up over the mountains late. It was delayed an hour out of Atlanta because of thunderstorms. Flights into Montana are often long and arduous. This one was no exception. They both planned on being at the office early the next day. The long flight was not going to make that any easier.

The meeting

Later that week, the FBI profilers arrived from Quantico to help out with the case. After a couple of days, Wilson was getting frustrated. He wanted specifics, but what he got was so general that it could fit *anyone* walking down the street. Wilson tried to tell them they weren't being specific enough, but they continued to pound the same old nail. Wilson thought it was a waste of time and money. He was spending day and night reading everything Bar Jonah had written, convinced the answer to Zach Ramsay's disappearance was buried in Bar Jonah's coded writings. The profilers seemed more interested in fitting Bar Jonah into some kind of behavioral schema that was yielding nothing. They stayed a little more than a week. Wilson said he was glad to see them go. They had used up valuable time. A kid was missing and presumed dead. A week after the profilers left Great Falls, Cameron received a ranting phone call from Wilson. When the members of the profile team returned to Quantico, they received a special commendation for their work on the Ramsay case. Wilson said they had done nothing but waste his time and yet they received an award. It pissed him off.

* * *

Rachel Howard was periodically getting phone calls from Cameron letting her know the status of the case. Even though he was convinced that Bar Jonah had killed and cannibalized Zach, Cameron hedged when he talked to Rachel. Rachel was convinced that Zach was still alive. Franz and Joan Cook had arranged everything and they had succeeded in keeping Zach hidden. He was probably in Africa. Rachel and the Ladies were continuing their efforts to discover clues to Zach's whereabouts. Each time Rachel got a new piece of evidence she drove from Choteau to Great Falls to meet with the Ladies. Each time they offered Rachel hope with new insights and psychic revelations of where Zach had been. Unfortunately, each time, like all the others, they had just missed him.

Rachel was becoming more quietly distraught with the updates from Cameron. What if it was true, Zach wasn't coming home? Rachel couldn't believe that. She had to meet Bar Jonah for herself.

* * *

The Cascade County Detention Center was crowded with family members waiting to see their loved ones whose lives were now owned by the state. For some it would only be a few months of incarceration. For a few others it would be life. Rachel got there just before the guards began walking wives, mothers, fathers, sisters and brothers and of course kids, through the metal detector portal. No beeps and you were good to go. A beep and they waved a magic wand over you. If they couldn't find the offending chunk of metal that was setting off the sensor, you could either be strip-searched or go home. Your choice. When Rachel arrived, she noticed that everyone

155

was wearing rubber flip-flops. She didn't know that visitors weren't allowed to wear shoes into the visiting area. Rachel had driven all of the way down from Choteau. She sure as hell didn't want to have to drive back without seeing Bar Jonah. Rachel noticed a woman who had a pair of flip-flops poking out of her tote bag. She also had another pair on her feet. Rachel walked over to the woman and told her she had forgotten her rubber shoes and wanted to know if she happened to have a spare pair. Rachel told her she had been sick and hadn't seen her husband in so long. She didn't want to miss visiting day. The woman said she thought that her sister was coming and she brought the extra pair for her. But since she wasn't there and Rachel had been sick, she guessed they were meant to be Rachel's. Rachel thanked her profusely, took her sneakers off and donned the flip-flops. She sat her shoes under a metal corrugated bench screwed to the floor. When she walked up to the guard, he asked whom she was there to see and what her relation to the inmate was. Bar Jonah was her brother, she said. She had come in from out of town to see him. When the guard ceremoniously waved Rachel through the rectangular flat black portal, the red signal light remained dim and the small conical shaped horn did not beep. The guard called back and alerted the jail staff that Bar Jonah had a visitor. Bar Jonah acted confused when the guard told him his sister was there to see him. Neither Bob nor Tyra had said anything about Lois flying in. He guessed that she wanted to surprise him.

* * *

A group of visitors were herded into a holding area, while the outside door was closed and locked. Rachel was standing in front of the flock in the small containment area. She was aware of the others standing behind her, craning their necks to see the bulging cycloptic eye, peering in from the visitors' area through the bulletproof wired glass. An obnoxious clang rang out in the containment area when the guard, after convincing himself that it was safe, slipped an eight-ounce polished metal skeleton key into a slot in the door, turned it once to the right, once to the left and then made a double-turn to the right again. The guard stepped back for a second and waited for the electronic latch in the door to activate. Then he pulled on the door, which Rachel could see opened heavily. No one tried to push or shove, they just followed the guard, who did not speak to anyone down the narrow hallway and into the visitors' section. There were several small square beige tables with bolted down benches scattered throughout. The tables were obviously welded to the floor. Rachel took one of the seats. A guard asked her whom she was waiting for. She said Bar Jonah.

A horseshoe-shaped bull pin with several television monitors and uniformed guards sat directly on Rachel's left. In a few seconds Rachel heard from an overhead speaker, "Bring in Bar Jonah." Through a locked door off to the right of the bull pin, a paint-scuffed door opened and a bulging, bellied man with long, greasy hair and a full, scraggly beard came through the door. Bar Jonah stood for a moment looking around for Lois. He was perplexed; she wasn't there. Then the guard accompanying Bar Jonah led him over to Rachel's bench. Rachel stood up and said, "I am Rachel Howard, Zachary Ramsay's mother."

* * *

Bar Jonah sat down at the bench, took his glasses off, rubbed his forehead and leaned as far back as he could without falling off of the bench. Rachel could see that he did not recognize her. He had never seen her before. She looked at Bar Jonah and said, "I am really good at seeing through someone's bullshit and I have one question for you. Did you kill my son?" Bar Jonah looked compassionately at Rachel, with tears welling in his reddening eyes and said in all earnestness, "*No …* I didn't hurt Zach. I never even met him." Rachel *knew* at that moment that Bar Jonah was telling her the truth. Then Bar Jonah began to tell her how he understood the pain she was

157

going through; he had been tortured and abused as a boy. He had an understanding that most others just didn't have. Rachel could see the anguish that tortured Bar Jonah's very soul. They didn't talk much more about Zach during the visit. Mostly they talked about God. Bar Jonah assured Rachel that he would pray for her and Zach. Moreover, he was a pretty good detective himself. Even though he was busy trying to clear his name, he would start looking into the case personally. Bar Jonah thought it would sure help if Rachel would write a letter to the prosecutor's office saying that she didn't think he had hurt Zach. It might help if she talked to Detectives Cameron and Theisen and Agent Wilson from the FBI too. Rachel said that she would. Then she thanked Bar Jonah for agreeing to see her. They stood up in unison and hugged under the watchful eyes of the guards in the bull pin. Right before Rachel walked away, Bar Jonah extended his right hand in friendship and assured her again that he would pray for her until Zach found his way home. He said he had a special relationship with God. God had performed many miracles for him when he was suffering, like Jesus suffered under Pontius Pilate. Bar Jonah would pray unceasingly for Zach's safe return. It wasn't a long visit but Rachel got what she came for. Bar Jonah was a good Christian man. He not only hadn't harmed Zach but Rachel knew in her heart that he wouldn't harm any child. And, most importantly for Rachel, there was now not a shred of doubt that Zach was alive.

* * *

Bar Jonah told the guard he would do anything for a cigarette and laughed as he sauntered back to his cell. Rachel looked better than the last time he had seen her at church, he thought. The snitch, who had whispered to Bar Jonah at the last minute that he was going to be getting a visit from the missing kid's mother, wanted to know how the visit had gone. He needed to get back to the guard who had told him right after he'd seen

158

Rachel in the waiting area. Bar Jonah lifted his eyes up from his Bible and assured the snitch that the visit had gone fine, "Just fine," he said.

Splitting

On May 12th, Cameron called Sherri and played her a portion of the interview tape with Pam. About a week later Sherri responded by sending Cameron a lengthy and rambling letter, that not only included her feelings about what Pam said on the tape, but also a short commentary about Georg Karl Grossman, a "post-WWII German degenerate that made a living selling human flesh." In her letter, Sherri also said that she thought that she sounded paranoid to other people, even though she took a blood test a little over a year before that showed that she didn't have schizophrenia.

Sherri told Cameron that an image had come to her of where Bar Jonah had dumped Zach's body. She didn't know Great Falls very well, so she had scoured a bunch of books at the library until she found a photograph that matched the image alive in her imagination. She made a copy of the photograph and mailed it to Cameron, instructing him to "… take the bush on the left of the picture and place it at the center of the picture where the shadows of the sun stop. Also take away the dead tree stumps next to it, on the right, at the edge of the sun shadow. The land that is lit by the sun is the 'gully' between some rising cliffs in the background. Also, the ground cover is more sparse. It's almost like a lone bush right near the edge of the drop off. Anyway, do you have any landscape like this anywhere around Great Falls? It's taken me all this time to find a photo that is even close. PLEASE let me know if you actually have any places like this around Great Falls … the horses, sunflowers, wide gully … I do like to keep track to see some sort of 'error' or 'confirmation' rate about the images that I see. I think you may be looking for a few more bodies than just the little boy. It's very possible. And, I think it's very possible Pam was 'involved,' but perhaps against her will ... like maybe she was around when something happened ... and that's how she knows about it all. I wish I could get more details from you. It does make it easier to focus, and I am quite capable of separating what you tell me from what I know and can testify to."

Sherri also wanted Cameron to help her get a job with law enforcement, which would allow her to use her psychic abilities to find missing persons. She was sure that the picture she sent him would point the case in the right direction. The remains of the kid's body should be scattered right around that general kind of area. The cops just had to find something that looked like it and go get Zach's body. It shouldn't be too hard to find. Sherri had given Cameron good directions.

* * *

Cameron, Wilson and Theisen were concerned about the possibility of using Pam and Sherri as witnesses. As far as they were concerned, they were both insane. What would a jury think of them? As soon as Pam started talking about voodoo and sacrificing small animals and Sherri started talking about her visions, they would be immediately discredited. The case could become a laughing stock and Bar Jonah could walk, again. Bar Jonah had already had one too many miracles.

* * *

A little earlier that same day, Bar Jonah sat in his cell and decided that he should write a letter to the two boys he had tried to murder in 1977. Bar Jonah was sure they had not forgiven him. He had forgiven them long ago for sending him to prison. Bar Jonah kept trying to get comfortable sitting on the edge of his metal bunk, but the mattress was so thin that one of the cheeks of his ass kept riding against the grated metal of the bed frame. He crossed his legs this way and that until he was finally able to prop the yellow pad on his thigh and write

160

the short note to each of the boys. *You need to forgive me. I am the force that lives inside you. The me that lives inside of you.* Bar Jonah liked to keep track of all the boys and some of the girls that he had made himself important to over the years. Just in case they ever needed him for anything, he would know where they were. The guard commented that the envelope was much thinner than most of Bar Jonah's other dozen or so letters that he mailed out every day. Bar Jonah told the guard he'd said all that he needed to say, explaining it wasn't how much you said that was important, but the sincerity of your thoughts.

CHAPTER NINE

The Interviews

By late June, the Bar Jonah case was also beginning to cull a lot of curiosity from some of the other officers. The gymnasium area wasn't secured and there was some question about some of the cops taking souvenirs from the stockpile of evidence. Cameron thought it would be a good idea to secure the area and wrote a memo to Lieutenant Carpenter:

From: Sgt. Cameron
Date: 6–21–00

I think it would be wise for us to restrict access to the South Drying Room that is used for evidence storage. It has always been a concern of mine. When we took this case over we put a lock on the door but the key is left in the door for anyone to access. A sign-in sheet on the outside of the door would be good and we could keep track of the access on the clerk's computer.

Other matters: The lab called at 1700 hours yesterday and identified the radial adolescent bone as human. It matches the other small bone fragments that were collected earlier. It is not Zach. We obviously have more than one victim and will have to do extensive research to find out who it is. This human bone was found only 6 inches down and mixed in with Bar Jonah's papers so I doubt this is an old burial site. We will also have to send in the other 11 bone fragments for comparison. This will be very expensive but the Chief is aware of this. All of Bar Jonah's motions were denied and trial is set for August. Preparation for this trial will be extensive and we have to win. I doubt that we will be charging him with Zach prior to August. The only way we would is if the other bones are Zach. I foresee this case tuning into a serial killer bucket of worms and becoming quite HUGE. I think it already has!!!!!!!!!!!!

Sgt. John Cameron

On June 28th, Cameron and Wilson started looking more closely at Bar Jonah's two heavy binders, filled with thousands of photographs of children. Bar Jonah also had dozens of packages of photographs, still with their negatives, that he hadn't yet placed in the binders. One package in particular caused concern for Cameron. The first few pictures were of a heavy-set Indian boy, lying on a heavily worn love seat. The boy was on his back with his shirt pulled up and his sweat pants pulled down, almost over his hips. The boy had his finger in his mouth. There were several other photographs of two other boys on the same 35 mm roll of film. Sandwiched between the photographs of the boys were pictures of Bar Jonah nude, lying back on his bed. His penis was erect and a massive scar was apparent on his right leg. Wilson commented that the size of Bar Jonah's penis was nothing to be proud of.

Cameron recognized the bigger boy as Roland and the younger, smaller boy as Stormy. Everyone knew them. They weren't bad boys; it's just that the cops would see them wandering all over the city. Never with a parent, always by themselves. Cameron commented to Theisen that the younger one was like a tornado. He'd just run around in circles like he was out of his head. Cameron and Wilson decided they would go and interview Roland the next morning.

* * *

At nine o'clock on the morning on the 29th of June, Gerald walked sleepy-eyed to the door of the apartment. Lori still hadn't gotten home from being out with her friends the night before. Gerald thought it was her knocking at the door. He was surprised instead to find a cop and an FBI agent. Cameron and Wilson told Gerald they were investigating Bar Jonah and had concerns that he may have sexually assaulted Roland and Stormy. Cameron pulled out one of the pictures of a third boy. Gerald said that was Stanley, but he had moved back up to the Fort Peck Reservation, so he wasn't there. Gerald agreed for Roland to be interviewed. He was still asleep but Cameron could go in and wake him up if he wanted.

Roland wasn't sure for a few minutes why the two men were standing in his bedroom. Even as Cameron began explaining the reason for them being there, Roland was still pretty foggy. Cameron asked Roland if he would be willing to come down to the police station and talk with him and Wilson about Bar Jonah. They could record the conversation so they wouldn't have to do it again. That way they'd be sure not to miss anything. Roland nodded that he would.

When they got to the police station, Wilson thought it would be best if Cameron interviewed Roland. He would listen and watch from outside of the interview room. Cameron started off the interview by telling Roland that he just wanted to get to know him and to find out how Bar Jonah had treated him. But they weren't there to trap Bar Jonah or to make up stories or anything like that. Roland initially began by telling Cameron that Bar Jonah was nice. Then Cameron started asking Roland about the pictures. As Roland became more at ease he told Cameron that Bar Jonah used to take a lot of pictures of him, Stormy and Stanley. Roland also said that Bar Jonah would handcuff his and Stanley's arms behind their backs like chicken wings. But they were real good friends too. Bob had even asked Roland to help him and Bar Jonah's mother clean out his apartment after he got arrested. That was okay, except that Bob scared him when he said that he'd better keep his mouth shut or social services might make him go and live somewhere else. "Just be careful" Bob told Roland. Roland told Lori and then she got afraid too and wouldn't let him and Stormy go outside. The social service people may pick them up and take them off somewhere. You can never tell. Bob and Tyra wanted to know if Bar Jonah had ever done anything like, *you know*, to any of the boys. Roland said that he told Bob and Tyra no. Cameron sat back quietly incensed at Bob's audacity. As the interview seemed to be winding down, Roland spoke up and said that Bar Jonah used to sit on top of them and make them cry. Cameron saw this as an opening and told Roland, "You know something, Roland, you can tell us—right here— anything that happened and we're not going to go, you know, an hour from now and tell step dad and tell your mother. We're not going to do that. Okay? Sometimes, you know, people don't want to get involved, they just want things to go away—but you know, in a case like this, with a guy like this—it'll never go away until the truth comes out. So if there's some things that Nathan did to you and did to Stanley, that maybe you haven't quite told us everything. It's all right because we're not going to go blabber mouth—and let everybody know. Okay?"

Cameron was lying. Not only was Wilson listening, so was Gerald. Cameron told Roland he wasn't in any trouble. He had done nothing wrong. Roland sat for a few seconds, when tears suddenly began streaming down his cheeks. At times, he was hard to understand because he tended to slur his words, especially when he started crying. Then the sobbing began as he started to tell Cameron what Bar Jonah had done.

166

During the interview, Roland didn't go into everything that had happened. Most of it he would forever keep to himself. Ultimately it would be Bar Jonah who would later reveal the details of what he had done to the boys that he considered like sons. Gerald stood listening, behind the one way glass becoming increasingly furious at Bar Jonah. It was good Bar Jonah was already in jail, otherwise Gerald would have killed him.

Roland sobbed and heaved for a full half-hour. He was inconsolable. Cameron kept wiping the tears out of his own eyes as he tried to comfort Roland. By now, it was just a little after noon. As soon as Roland left the interview room, Cameron, Wilson and Theisen left for Fort Peck to interview Stanley.

When they arrived at the reservation, Cameron commented that the place looked like a Beirut war zone. It had the look of being dismal and bombed out. Nothing had seen a coat of fresh paint in years. There wasn't even a police or sheriff's department. If Stanley agreed to be interviewed, where in the hell would they do it? Other than a bar that doubled as a gas station, the only other building was the Fraser public school. On the way to Stanley's, Cameron pulled into the parking lot, copied the emergency number off of the door and called the school janitor, who agreed to let them use the library to do the interview. Cameron told the janitor that Stanley was not in trouble; he had done nothing wrong. He just might have some information about a case that they could use in an investigation.

* * *

Tanya Big Leggins answered the door dressed in gray stretch pants that barely contained the rolls of fat that lurched in every direction. Her watery, pendulous breasts made her soup-stained sweatshirt ride far up above her bulging abdomen, showing the finger-wide stretch marks that had taken their toll on Tanya's belly.

Tanya was understandably suspicious. Two whites on the res looking for her kid. Lori had called Tanya and let her know

Cameron and Wilson were on their way up. She just said it involved Bar Jonah, but she didn't go into any details with Tanya. It didn't matter. These were cops and they were white. Stanley said he would talk with Cameron and Wilson, but he didn't want it to take too long.

* * *

Tanya and Stanley pulled in right behind Cameron and Wilson. The janitor was walking around in the parking lot wondering what took them so long to get there. He had understood they were coming right away. Once the janitor unlocked the door, Stanley led them down to the library. Cameron unpacked the video camera he brought to film the interview. It was a cumbersome VHS recorder that the Great Falls Police used to record crime scenes and document evidence. A few of the cops had gotten into trouble for not watching their mouth at crime scenes, saying things best unsaid and having it picked up on the tape. That didn't happen once they discovered the recorder had a dangling plug that they could shove into the microphone to block sound.

Cameron set the recorder up on the chrome tripod, angled it toward the three chairs and started the tape rolling. Cameron began the interview, asking perfunctory questions to try to put Stanley more at ease as he seemed subdued and withdrawn. When Cameron showed Stanley some of the same photographs he had shown Roland, he seemed to become slightly more interested. Curious even. Cameron began asking Stanley if Bar Jonah had ever touched him inappropriately, in a sexual way. Stanley tearfully said that Bar Jonah had. Bar Jonah also tried to hang him in the kitchen with a rope. He had it strung through some kind of hook in the ceiling. Stanley was sniffing hard and deep, trying to contain his tears. Cameron and Wilson tried to assuage Stanley's pain and embarrassment. Like Roland, Stanley sobbed for at least half an hour.

After Stanley stopped crying, Cameron got up and checked the video. When Cameron rewound the tape, a small two inch fold-out screen from the side of the video camera allowed him to see that the interview had been recorded successfully. He was relieved.

Wilson looked up, saw Cameron frustratedly fiddling with some of the controls and asked him if something was wrong. Then he heard Cameron say "Oh fuck." There was *no* sound. Cameron had forgotten to take out the mic plug. They would have to do the interview over. Stanley was enraged. "I'm not going to fucking do it," he kept saying. Cameron and Wilson tried to console Stanley, but he would have none of it. He just wanted to go the fuck home. Cameron grabbed another chair and brought Tanya into the room. They clearly needed help. After a few minutes of talking with Stanley, Tanya was able to coach him into going through the motions of being interviewed again. But Stanley was still pissed and agitated. Cameron and Wilson got the interview and Stanley saying on tape, with sound, that Bar Jonah had tried to hang him and had sexually assaulted him. But the interview looked staged and scripted. Cameron knew he would be questioned in court about the mistake with the mic plug, but he did not see it as an insurmountable problem. Although the interview had to be redone, it didn't change the fact of what Bar Jonah had done to Stanley.

* * *

It was happy birthday time again for Roland. But nothing could compare with the birthday he had had just a year before with Bar Jonah. That was the birthday he would never forget. Roland still told his friends about the best birthday ever, when his belly bounced up and down as he tried to outrun the flaming M-80, throwing himself headfirst across the hood of Bar Jonah's car just like a major leaguer sliding into home plate, and Bar Jonah grabbing him by his shirt collar, spinning him around like a big top just in time to see the wax can explode way up into the night sky.

* * *

When he talked about that birthday night, Roland's thick, squared off chest would shiver with so much excitement, then right at the end, as he squeezed out the last few words, he sounded like a calliope losing its happy wind. Most of all though, Roland remembered going out to eat right before he and Bar Jonah went to shoot off the fireworks. And even more than anything else in the whole world, Roland would never ever forget when Bar Jonah called him *his* boy at Evelyn's All You Can Eat smorgasbord.

The first thing Cameron did when Lori answered the door was to apologize for showing up on July 4th. But he needed to talk with Roland for just a few minutes. He had met with Stanley a couple of days before up in Fraser, Cameron said, and he needed to talk to Roland about a couple of things. It wouldn't take very long though. Roland was sitting on the couch when Cameron was talking with Lori at the front door. He got up, walked over, shook Cameron's hand and told Lori that he would go talk with Cameron. Lori said she would drive Roland on down to the police station.

Cameron met Lori and Roland in the lobby of the GFPD. They took the elevator, rattletrap that it was, to the second floor and went into a faded green room with three straight-back chairs and a gouged-up oak table. Cameron only had three questions, but he needed to get Roland's answers on tape. Did Roland call Stanley and let him know the cops were coming to talk to him and if he did, did Roland tell Stanley what the cops wanted to talk to him about? Cameron also wanted to know if Roland and Stanley had rehearsed their stories about Bar Jonah. Roland told Cameron that he did call Stanley. Really he said, Lori had called Tanya and told her that the cops were coming up to Fraser to talk to Stanley about Bar Jonah. But

170

Roland told Cameron that Lori hadn't said anything about why the cops wanted to talk to Stanley. Just that he wasn't in *no* trouble. After Lori had gotten through talking to Tanya, she handed the phone to Roland. Roland told Stanley the cops were coming to talk to him about Bar Jonah, but he wouldn't tell him about what.

When Cameron told Roland about what Stanley had said that Bar Jonah did to him, Roland again began sobbing. He was sorry he had said anything at all. He hadn't wanted to be the one who made Bar Jonah go back to prison. Roland also muttered through his deep sobs, that he didn't want social services to take him and Stormy away from Lori. He didn't want to have to go live somewhere else, probably with a white family. Cameron looked cock-eyed at Roland, not understanding what he was talking about. There had never been any discussion about calling social services and taking the kids away from Lori. When Cameron told Roland that there was no reason to do anything like that, Roland said that Bob and Bar Jonah had told him to keep his mouth shut. If he didn't, Bar Jonah would get sent back to prison, this time forever and then social services would come and take him and all of his brothers and sisters away and make them go live with a white family. Cameron tipped the gray chair back against the wall and balanced the teetering legs with the back of his shiny head. He wasn't surprised by Bar Jonah's brazenness, but he was by Bob's. Cameron thought that Bob would do anything to protect Bar Jonah and undermine the investigation. But he had to keep playing Bob, if he expected to continue to get any cooperation at all. The whole interview lasted only eighteen minutes. Cameron told Roland to wait in the echoey room while he went out and made a quick call.

Before Cameron opened the door and walked back into the interview room, he stood for a moment and looked at Roland through the wire-latticed glass in the door. Cameron thought Roland was slouching over in the gunmetal chair. But as he stood there a while longer, Cameron realized that Roland's belly was so rotund, that it looked like he had a heavy stone slung around his neck, folding him in two like a collapsed rag doll.

Cameron had seen Lori in the hallway as he had been walking back to the interview room. Lori had been meeting with Theisen, confirming that she had not said anything to her sister about why the cops were coming up to Fraser to talk to Stanley. Cameron leaned down and told Lori that he had arranged a ride for Roland, if that was okay: she wouldn't have to take him back home. Lori nodded, saying it was okay with her.

When Cameron opened the door to the interview room, Roland raised his head and asked if he could go ahead and leave. It was his birthday and he didn't want to spend it at the police station. Cameron told him yes, they were finished and that he would walk out with him. When they got to the front door of the police station, a Great Falls Police cruiser, with its lights flashing, was waiting for Roland. The patrol officer walked up to Roland and put his hand on his shoulder and told him to hop in, he was going to take him back home in style. Roland started laughing and said out loud that this might be his second best birthday ever as he feigned dodging the untamed red and blue javelins of light trying to harpoon him. Roland's overjoyed eyes pushed open their droopy lids and kept looking back at Cameron as the police car sped away. Right before Roland turned his head around, he saw Cameron waving his hand. In that second, Roland's dull, pale yellow teeth seemed to brighten a bit in the beaming sunlight. Roland laughed deep from in his belly, threw his hand in the air and started waving back and forth like a windshield wiper, trying to outdo Cameron.

The cruiser quickly pulled out onto River Road. Just for fun, Roland asked the officer if he could turn on his siren. When the officer looked around, there wasn't another car to be seen. So, for a brief, but important second, the police officer flipped on the siren. The policeman said he couldn't leave the siren on because it's really only for emergencies, but he sure hoped Roland liked hearing it. Roland was so excited that he couldn't even talk. He just kept shaking his head and bouncing up and down in the seat. Right before they got back to Lori's, Roland told the officer that he might want to become a U.S. Marshal after all. As the patrol officer pulled back out onto 10th Ave., he shook his head at how sad and desperate a kid Roland was. Roland was one of those kids that the cop didn't know where he was going to end up.

* * *

As Cameron, Theisen and Wilson continued to work together, Cameron and Theisen began to resent Wilson. It wasn't an intense resentment but it was there. Wilson got paid three times as much working for the Feds than Cameron or Theisen made together. But more than that, he wouldn't have to go through the bullshit of testifying in court. Wilson was only assisting the local police department; it wasn't a federal case. They didn't have any problems with Wilson, it was just the way the system was. Wilson got to benefit from it; Cameron and Theisen didn't. The good thing was that Wilson was able to bring more resources to bear on the investigation than Cameron or Theisen.

Corky Groves was continuing to demand that Cameron close the case. It was eating up too much of the department's money and resources. Moreover, Groves believed that Bar Jonah wasn't guilty; Rachel Howard was. Bellusci was still in the background, urging Groves to refocus the investigation back to Rachel. The other cops were increasingly resenting Cameron and Theisen for only having to manage the Bar Jonah case. Theisen was really beginning to feel the pressure. He was beginning to drink more and wake up in the middle of the night screaming. Laurie, Theisen's wife, was determined that Bar Jonah was not going to destroy her marriage the way

Cameron's marriage was crumbling apart. No matter what happened, she was determined to keep things together until Bar Jonah was convicted. Theisen only had a couple of years to go before he had his twenty years on the force. But it seemed like Groves was doing everything he could to get rid of him early. Cameron and Theisen started talking about their night sweats and middle of the night outbursts. They both knew that the further they got into the investigation the worse it was going to get.

* * *

The circle of indignation

About three p.m. on July 5th, Cameron and Theisen showed up at the jail, telling the guard on duty they wanted to see Bar Jonah. A few minutes later, Cameron and Theisen walked into the holding cell and found Bar Jonah sitting, with his legs crossed, his eyes catching Cameron's, insinuating a familiarity that wasn't there. Cameron looked away. Bar Jonah stood up and extended his hand as a symbol of friendship and no hard feelings. Cameron reached out and slid into Bar Jonah's hand an indictment for the sexual assault of Roland, Stanley and Stormy, kidnapping and assault with a weapon. The first count alone carried a possible 100 year sentence for each boy. You have been served, Mr. Bar Jonah, Cameron said. Then he and Theisen walked out the door. Bar Jonah stood for a minute and read the indictment. He was seething. He yelled for the guard to take him back to his cell immediately. A half-hour later, a guard showed up to a pacing Bar Jonah, who demanded to know why the guard took so long to respond. The guard smiled at Bar Jonah, took him by the arm and escorted him back to his cell, never speaking. As soon as Bar Jonah sat down on his bed he took out a long yellow legal pad and wrote Roland, Stanley and Stormy a letter:

Dear Roland, Stanley and Stormy,

I read the court document today and I couldn't believe you kids hate me so much. All 3 of you know I didn't do anything to you guys. Detective Cameron must of really scared you guys and I'm looking at 3 life sentences—death in prison. That isn't going to happen because if you receive this then I'm dead. I either killed myself or someone has killed me. But all of you know I've always treated you and the boys really well. I just hope someday you boys can forgive yourself. I've already prayed to God that he'll forgive you too. YOU CAN CLEAR MY NAME.

Love, Bar Jonah

Bar Jonah addressed the envelope to Roland and licked it with an extra dose of spit, telling one of the other inmates that he wanted to give the boys a little something extra of himself. The other inmate looked suspiciously at Bar Jonah, thinking he was a freak among freaks.

When Roland ripped open the letter the next day, he tried to read it but couldn't. He had gotten to be a better reader, but not good enough to read a whole letter by himself. Especially some of the big words, those really confused him. Roland took the letter to Lori, who read it to him. As soon as Lori read the part about Bar Jonah being dead, Roland began crying. He'd killed him. Roland never wanted Bar Jonah to get hurt. He was just telling the truth about what Bar Jonah had done. Bar Jonah had been like a dad to him and now he'd killed him. Lori tried to reassure Roland that Bar Jonah wasn't dead. He was only acting like he was dead, because he wanted Roland to take back what he had said and tell the cops Bar Jonah really didn't do anything to him. Roland felt miserable. Lori called the jail and asked if Bar Jonah was dead. The sheriff deputy who took the call asked Lori to repeat herself a couple of times; he couldn't understand the thick Indian cadence in her voice, plus Lori always added "init" at the end of every sentence. Initially the deputy thought Lori might have been making a death threat against Bar Jonah. He then realized that she just wanted to know if Bar Jonah was alive or dead. The deputy told her Bar Jonah was very much alive. At that moment he was trying out a new trivia game that he was working on with a couple of the other prisoners. When Lori told Roland that Bar Jonah was okay, he stood up and started storming off down the hallway. Right before he slammed his bedroom door, Roland yelled back to Lori that he wasn't going to court to testify against Bar Jonah. No way.

* * *

After Roland got the letter from Bar Jonah, Lori had had enough. It was time to move back to Fraser. Time to take her kid back up to the far northeast corner of Montana to be with his own people. He was starting to smart off to Lori. Roland was a good boy; he hadn't done much mouthing off. He'd always been respectful to his mother. Lori thought it was all getting to be too much for him. It was time to take him back home.

* * *

A week later Lori and Gerald had packed up the kids, moved back to Fraser and were living with Tanya. The following week Roland started getting dizzy and losing his balance. The doctor that came to the res once a week poked Roland in the arm with a needle. He had good fat blue veins that popped up real good off of his brown skin and they didn't roll. The blood flowed freely through the shiny needle into the red, rubber-capped glass tube. A few days later, the public health nurse called and told Lori that Roland was diabetic. He didn't need to have shots yet, but they weren't too far off. He was going to need to watch his diet real careful because the doctor didn't want Roland to start getting the sugar real bad at such a young age. Later, Lori told Tanya the doctor had called it juvenile diabetes. Lori also said that Roland was still having a bad time, knowing that the

176

cops were going to make him say what Bar Jonah had done to him in court and that he would be the one who sent Bar Jonah back to prison. Some of the Big Leggins that were serving time in the state penitentiary were already talking about gutting Bar Jonah if he got convicted. Word was getting back to Roland that if Bar Jonah went to prison he'd be killed. Stanley had started blabbing around the res what Bar Jonah had done to him and Roland. It wasn't very long before Roland's cousins started calling him queer and cock sucker. They didn't seem to pick on Stanley, but maybe that was because Stanley was the one who usually led the charge against Roland.

It wouldn't be long before school started up again and Roland wanted to do good. His grades in Great Falls had fallen behind even though he had been in special classes. He was worried about being able to do well because he was going to start getting into fights if his cousins didn't stop teasing him. They had talked around so much that other kids at school also started calling him queer. Word was getting out back in Great Falls about Bar Jonah. The newspapers were saying that Bar Jonah had abused some boys. The cops were saying that he'd killed and eaten the kid that disappeared back in '96. One of his cousins even said that the reason Roland got sugar was because he ate some of the meat from the dead kid that Bar Jonah had butchered.

Roland spent most of his days hiding inside the trailer, watching television and not talking to anyone but Stormy. Lori took Roland to a psychotherapist who was with the Indian Health Center and went from res to res. She said it was best to get Roland away from the constant tormenting by the other kids. It was especially hard on Roland because it was his family who was tormenting him. Lori didn't want Roland to have to endure any more pestering, so she packed up Roland with the rest of the kids and moved on down to Billings. It wouldn't be but a few weeks before Roland and Stormy could start school there. Billings had a lot of really nice casinos too. They had the best payouts in the state. Lori figured she'd be luckier in the bigger city too.

* * *

Wilson contacted Quantico and said he wanted someone to come in and start cataloging the items taken from Bar Jonah's apartment. They were just tossed in unlabeled boxes and stored randomly at the police department. A few days later, three evidence technicians from the FBI arrived in Great Falls to catalog every item taken from Bar Jonah's, down to the smallest scraps of paper. The document turned out to be a 15,000 item database.

* * *

Bar Jonah sat in his cell waiting for deliverance from his captors. A divine commission would be brought about by the volition of God. It would come any day now. He was proclaiming his innocence to anyone who would listen, about the lies the boys had made up about him. Cameron was also fabricating a pack of lies against him about killing Zach. If he were charged, he'd be facing the death penalty. But it was hard to get a conviction without a body. As Bar Jonah said many times, "There is no body." When Bar Jonah felt any despair, he would remember Psalm 77:14: *You are the God who performs miracles.* After reciting verse 14 over and over again, Bar Jonah would lie back on his cot, drift off to sleep and begin dreaming.

* * *

Cameron continued to get more worked up over the case. Not just the case, but also the failures of the police and the court system that had allowed Bar Jonah to not only get out in the first place, but had also failed to put him back behind bars. In late July Cameron called Patrick Flaherty and asked him if he would be willing to talk to him privately. He wanted to know if Bar Jonah had confessed to killing Zach back in 1996 when

Flaherty represented him. Cameron also had pulled the file on the Shawn Watkins case and was appalled. Flaherty told Cameron he couldn't discuss anything about a former client with him. Cameron, pissed off, sat down and wrote Flaherty a letter:

Dear Pat,

I had a chance to review the entire file on the Shawn Watkins case and find myself wondering how the entire law enforcement, courts and legal community could have failed in the way we failed Zachary Ramsay. I was sick to my stomach after reading the sex offender evaluation done by Interconnections Counseling Group. I have read all of Bar Jonah's evaluations dating back to 1975 and cannot understand how this man slipped through the system repeatedly over 25 years. I take responsibility for thinking, in 1996, that Zachary was just a runaway. Our department must take responsibility for not pursuing Mr. Bar Jonah in 1996. The legal community must take its responsibility also. When the truth comes out on what occurred on February 6, 1996, this community will be shocked and dismayed at our failures. I don't think that Rachel Howard will ever believe Zachary is dead until I can produce a piece large enough to show her that this is what's left of Zachary. This will never happen. Mr. Bar Jonah dressed like a policeman and kidnapped Zachary as he walked to school on the morning of the Good Guy Breakfast. He then took Zachary to his garage where he raped him, strangled him and then cut him into pieces to hide the evidence. The previous detectives involved in this case knocked on his door within hours of Zachary disappearing. They *never* went back and our department must take its responsibility for that. Mr. Bar Jonah called you and spoke with you about going to the

179

police department and speaking with the detectives. Of course you represented your client as you should have and told him not to. Mr. Bar Jonah then consumed the flesh of Zachary Ramsay and made food out of him, probably feeding him to people that he despised over the years. This was the ultimate revenge. I should not even be sharing this case with you but I do in hopes that if there is anything you know, about the whereabouts of any of the remains of Zachary Ramsay, please let someone know. This case will destroy a lot of people in this community when it finally comes to a close. Thank you for your time.

Sgt. John A. Cameron

* * *

The case was now taking on a different momentum, particularly for Cameron. He was pushing. He knew he had Bar Jonah for the sexual assaults of Roland, Stanley and Stormy but he wanted to find Zach's body and put closure to a case that had haunted Great Falls. The media was having a blitzkrieg with the reports leaking out of the police department. Bar Jonah was being referred to as the cannibal killer. Lois and her family were being assaulted by reporters. Film crews from local and national media were camping out in front of the Foshays' home in Dudley. Lois's husband Lee was a defense contractor. There was talk going around to terminate some of his contracts because of the bad press being rained down on the family. Everyone wanted a story. The most cogent information came out of Great Falls itself by reporter Kim Skornogoski. On Sunday, August 6th, Skornogoski published the first major story on Bar Jonah on the front page, under the headline "The System Failed." She had gone into great detail about Bar Jonah's past history of molestation and assault and Massachusetts's abysmal incompetence in releasing Bar Jonah.

Cameron and Theisen were continuing to be pressured by Chief Jones and Lieutenant Groves. The resources were running thin; the money simply wasn't there. They were both raising hell. Groves, in particular, wouldn't take the pressure off. He was relentless in demanding the case be brought to an end. Jones said publicly that the department had spent between $150,000 and $200,000 to investigate the Ramsay case alone since February 1996. The cost of the DNA tests on the bone fragments was more than $50,000. The FBI was now fanning out and looking for possible victims in other locations where Bar Jonah had lived. They couldn't keep this up.

* * *

Cameron was now beginning to track down some of the other people that he found notes from or names scribbled on pieces of paper. One of the most intriguing was a note from Doc Bauman to Bar Jonah, "Thanks for the deer meat, greatly appreciated."

Knock, knock. Who's there?

Doc was sitting in his Christmas and Halloween living room, staring aimlessly out the window and daubing his tea bag around the rim of the delightfully decorated bone china cup that he was tenuously balancing in his lap. He had his left leg propped up on a red and green Santa-faced footstool. The weight of Doc's swollen leg was puffing up Santa's embossed, rosy chubby cheeks, making them curl up around his spindly pallid calf. For the past week Doc had been having problems with phlebitis. The doctor told him that he should stay off of the leg as much as possible. If a clot broke loose, it could go to his heart and kill him. "Let's watch it," the doctor said, "and see if it will go down with some blood thinners." Doc was good with that. He would prefer not to have the veins in his legs stripped.

The teacup poised in Doc's lap began to tremble, when he looked out the window and saw Cameron pull up in front of his house. Doc knew Cameron was a cop. He had run into him when he was arrested back in '93. It was just a matter of time before the police came snooping around. It had been a mistake ever getting involved with Bar Jonah in the first place. It was not only because Bar Jonah had robbed him of his one true love but also because Doc knew that the cops would start badgering him. They had never found Zach's body and Doc knew they never would. Doc had heard that Cameron was the kind of dog who would never stop digging for a bone. Once he got a sniff, he would paw around until he found something. Doc knew Cameron was going to be annoying. Until the mess that Bar Jonah had created was over, Doc's tea time was going to be intruded upon by Cameron's incessant hounding.

There were a dozen or so little Dutch boys adorned in pretty pointy hats and wooden shoes, dancing around the white porcelain teacup that Doc had resting on his lap. Doc reached under the delicate saucer, lifted it gingerly and sat it on the orange pumpkin table sitting within easy reach of his comfy chair. Then, when Doc heard Cameron's knuckles rap at his door, he pressed the little spring-loaded black button on the ash-smudged chrome ashtray that always sat beside his chair and pushed his cigarette through the waiting hole. He turned his head and spit a few flakes of tobacco that still lingered on his lips from his filterless cigarette.

* * *

A vile, yellow Scotch mist enveloped Doc's German style gingerbread house. When Cameron opened the screeching wooden gate, with its tall picket peaks, he found his feet not wanting to step one in front of the other, as he made his way to Doc's door. He was not afraid, only repulsed by the ambience of the house.

The reek as he was walking up the sidewalk was making him nauseous. Even Cameron's fist seemed to hesitate before it knocked on Doc's door. When Cameron pulled his clenched hand away from the door, he wiped it against his pants.

Doc reached down, lifted his left leg off Santa's face and pushed himself up with the right arm of the easy chair. He picked up his walnut cane, holding it for a moment, looking at it longingly, regretting that he had had to take off the soft pink faux fur that had adorned it for so long. Now though, he needed the extra support. The faux fur had delighted him so and attracted so many curious comments. But now alas, he could not take the chance of the pink fluffy fur slipping down the shaft and getting caught under the cane's rubber tip. Old people didn't live very long once they broke their hips. Doc hobbled on the cane, flinching with pain when he put too much weight on his left leg. He had thought about just yelling for Cameron to come on in but that would give him far too much of an advantage. Doc would answer his own door.

Cameron was struck by Doc's frailty when the door opened. Doc stood cocked to one side, holding himself feebly as he hopefully leaned on the cane. "Yes," Doc said, his quixotic eyes trying to outwit Cameron's ocular parry. Doc dropped his chin to his chest, exhaled wearily and coughed hoarsely, calling for phlegm to rise in his throat, hoping that another form of help-lessness would convey his innocence.

Cameron flashed his badge at Doc and told him that he was there because he had found a note that Doc had written to Bar Jonah. Doc looked long; he had no idea what Cameron was talking about. The note about the deer meat, Doc pondered for a moment. "Ahhh," Doc said, "Yes, now I recall. Please come in. You must pardon me, I am having some problems with my leg. Old age, I suspect. I'm just not as agile as I use to be." Doc swept his head to the left, pushed back hard against the blemished front door that had been disfigured by the years of

183

neglect and scraped a tall pile of fresh cat shit with the door sweep, streaking it across the oily, yellow-filmed hardwood floor. Doc had to pull on the edge of the door several times to break the suction of the shit that was sucking it into the saffron colored wall.

When Cameron walked into Doc's Christmas palace living room, the burnt ammonia stench that seemed to live like an alien entity inside the house almost overtook him. His stomach heaved like he was going to vomit from the fetidness of the thick air. Doc ceremoniously waved his hand for Cameron to sit down. In between short, gasping breaths, Cameron said he would stand. Cameron had the sense that he didn't know where he was. He was surrounded by the ungodly overwhelming odor of floor-to-ceiling swells of cat shit; everything was coated like fallout in a dried, mustard colored dust. Hundreds of photographs of anonymous boys adorned the walls. All the boys in the pictures were fully dressed. Some were in sports poses; others were sitting on a rock by a river. The same rock, the same river, a different boy. Under some of the photos were small slips of paper, with "A little elf" or "My spooky goblin" written with the rounded tip of a fat pencil. The ambience of the room was set out in a gaudy Halloween and Christmas entwined motif. Here lived a thousand Christmases with thousands of dolls, trucks and guns, dancing bears and stuffed animals, still wrapped up tightly in brittle opaque plastic.

Doc plopped himself back down in the chair that bore a well-worn impression of his butt, looked up at Cameron and exasperatedly asked how he could help. "I am not a well man," Doc said to Cameron. "Please, might we keep this short?" Cameron was unfazed. He began asking Doc pointed questions about his and Bar Jonah's relationship. Had he known Zach? When did Bar Jonah give Doc the deer meat? Doc reached over and wrapped the fingers of his right hand around the curved handle of his cane, lifted it over the arm of the chair and rested its indented rubber tip on the floor between

184

his pink slipper-covered feet. He raised himself slightly and sat his chin on top of the knuckles of both hands that were stacked one on top of the other, wrapped around the handle of his cane. Doc squinted his eyelids as he raised them high in their sockets, readying himself to answer Cameron's questions. His memory was cobwebby. He may have met Zach at some time in the past. It was difficult to say. Doc met so many boys. He was but a mere overgrown boy himself. All Cameron had to do was to look around, to see how much Doc was now able to enjoy the things that he had never been able to have in his youth. He was originally from Texas, close to the Mexican border. He had grown up very poor. Now in his twilight years he preferred to think about only pleasant things. That was why he surrounded himself with the spirit of Christmas, the pumpkins of Halloween and the bunnies of Easter. He liked his life to be very simple. Doc's chin was still resting on his white knuckles, which were now gripping the handle of the cane tighter and tighter. Cameron could see Doc's hands pulsing, as he squeezed … and unsqueezed them, over and over. When Doc spoke, his chin pushed his head up and down, making his false teeth clack and his mouth move like an out-of-tune cam driven by a secret hand that had slipped itself into the back of his neck. The slight tremor hanging onto the end of his words betrayed Doc's fear that Cameron's arrival was going to complicate his life.

The more questions that Cameron asked, the more reticent Doc became. Why, Doc implored, would Cameron take such an accusatory attitude with him. He did not understand. Of course Bar Jonah had been his friend. But he knew nothing about Bar Jonah's antics. Bar Jonah had given him some meat, yes, but he gave many people food. He was known for his generosity. Cameron struck Doc as a very difficult man. Doc would have been happy to help Cameron if he knew anything, which he didn't, but Cameron must be more respectful. After all he was a retired physician and deserved respect, if nothing else, for

185

the lives he had saved. Even when Bellusci had arrested Doc on those trumped-up charges in '93, he was more respectful in his tone than Cameron.

Cameron was getting exasperated with Doc's feigning naiveté. For a moment he had to suppress an impulse to jerk Doc up out of his chair and slap the shit out of him. Doc had to know more than he was saying, otherwise the ruse he was putting on wouldn't have been necessary. The question was how much did he know and how to go about squeezing it out of him. Cameron decided the best way was to appeal to Doc's conceit.

Doc sat and stared at Cameron, waiting for more questions that he could deny having any knowledge of. Cameron held his nose and asked Doc to show him around his house. He ignored the cat shit and told Doc he had never seen so many toys. Doc smiled and said he had spent his life collecting them. They were worth a great deal of money. Doc reached out for Cameron to help him out of his chair. Cameron turned his head away, pretending he didn't see Doc's come-and-help-me hand. When Cameron turned his head back around, he saw Doc pushing himself up with the curved handle of his walnut cane. As Doc stepped from between the Santa stool and his chair, he began hobbling across the floor, indicating with his head for Cameron to follow him. Doc left the scent of cheap aftershave and dry smoke in his wake as he crossed Cameron's path.

* * *

They made their way through the interconnecting archways, going from room to room, careening around the cat shit like it wasn't there. Doc was serving as master of ceremonies. His house was his theatre and the thousands of dolls were his audience. Doc was treating Cameron as a fellow celebrity by giving him the back stage tour. As they walked among the panoply, Cameron noticed how Doc adeptly avoided the cat shit with the round rubber tip of his cane. Cameron also

186

noticed for the first time that Doc painted his fingernails. Doc would sometimes stop, point with the tip of his cane and comment on a particular doll or picture of a boy hanging on one of the walls. He loved his home and being surrounded by his most precious possessions. It was his sanctuary. When they made their way around the final turn and ended up at the back door, Doc told Cameron that he was tired. Could they continue another time? He was in great pain. He was probably going to take some pain medication, sit and rest the remainder of the day. However, now that Doc knew that Cameron was seeking information about Bar Jonah, he would give it some thought. If he came up with anything that he thought was important, he would call Cameron straight away. Doc glanced down at the pile of cat shit blocking the back door and nonchalantly suggested that Cameron leave the same way he arrived. A few steps past a grease-caked stove, they were greeted by a grinning jack-o-lantern. "Thank you for coming, officer," Doc said. "I will be in touch if I think of anything that could be helpful." Cameron's stern eyes looked at Doc in riposte and told him that he could be sure they would be talking again.

As Cameron pulled the door closed behind him he heard Doc say, "Remember detective, the quality of mercy is not strained." Without being obvious Cameron walked as fast as he could to his car. He drove straight home, walked up the sidewalk past his garage and went into his screened-in porch. Cameron ripped his clothes off and tossed them out the back door onto the lawn. Then he went in, got into the shower and tried to scrub the stench off his body before he went back to the station.

* * *

After Doc saw Cameron drive away, he hooked the crook of his cane on his arm and walked back over to his chair. He sat down, propped his leg back up and lit a cigarette. He drew the warm, soothing smoke deep into his lungs. Then his face flushed to the point of tears. Doc reached into his shirt pocket, felt the end of his daisy-embossed handkerchief and twisted it into a tiny figure eight. When a drop of snot fell from his nostril onto his hand, Doc raised the cloth to his red spider-veined nose and dabbed it daintily. Doc slowly turned his head from side to side, his vision obscured by his now wet eyes. Everything in his cherished room seemed to be crying with him. Even the Santa tapestry that covered the wall beside the front door seemed to be as sad as Doc. Doc wrapped the ends of the handkerchief around his index finger and softly touched the corners of his eyes. When he pulled the cloth away, he saw that his make-up had smeared. He sighed and leaned back in his chair, thinking that sometimes he felt like such a little girl.

Lining things up

Wilson went to see Rachel and asked her for something of Zach's that would help him get an idea of who Zach was as a kid. Rachel, initially hesitant, agreed to give Wilson a black spiral bound notebook that had drawings and letters in strange combinations that had belonged to Zach. Wilson was struck by the drawings that depicted long claw-like fingernails and demons. He thought it might be a good idea to have the notebook checked for fingerprints. But the book came back from the FBI lab without showing any trace of Bar Jonah's fingerprints. The pages of the book were stained with a light purple dye and soft white dust. Wilson labeled and bagged the notebook in a large manila envelope and forgot about it for a long time.

Rachel was now more convinced than ever that Zach was alive. Her faith felt unshakable. She and the Ladies worked almost every day and night piecing together new clues about Franz and Joan Cook. Their evidence was building. But there was no one they could count on to investigate what they were finding out. They would have to go it alone or continue to believe that the Lord would someday lead Zach home. When He did, Rachel would be waiting for him with open arms.

* * *

In a large box that Bar Jonah had stuffed with hundreds of scraps of paper and letters, Cameron found the eviction letter Bar Jonah had written to Barry. Cameron had known Barry from having picked him up as a juvenile. He had been a passive little punk most of his life, always in some kind of trouble. Cameron wanted to talk to Barry.

Barry was living in an apartment that was even more run down than Bar Jonah's. When Barry answered the door, he looked at Cameron and straightaway said he didn't have anything to do with touching those kids. Bar Jonah did that shit. He went on saying that he had tried to tell Bar Jonah but he wouldn't listen. He'd gone back to his bedroom that night and just stayed the fuck out of it. But he didn't do nothing. Cameron hadn't even told Barry why he was there.

Barry laid it out for Cameron. Telling him how Bar Jonah had slept in the same bed with the boys that lived upstairs. Barry tried to tell Bar Jonah that he was going to get into trouble, but he wasn't someone who would listen to you. Cameron told Barry everything he had said was on the record and that he would be called to testify. When Barry started to put up a fuss, Cameron asked him why he didn't help Stanley when Bar Jonah was hanging him in the kitchen. Barry hung his sleepy eyes low and told Cameron he was ashamed of himself that he let Bar Jonah do what he did to the boys. But he was afraid of Bar Jonah. Everyone who knew Bar Jonah was afraid of him. What happens if he testifies and Bar Jonah gets off? Cameron assured Barry that Bar Jonah was never going to get out of prison. "He'll die in prison," Cameron said.

A few days later Bar Jonah got word in jail that Cameron had talked to Barry and he was going to testify that Bar Jonah had molested and tried to kill the boys. Bar Jonah slipped the stoolie that gave him the information a pack of cigarettes and sat down to write Barry a letter.

Dear Barry,

You know I didn't touch those kids. But you also know that I lied to the cops about the girl who said that you raped her. I gave you an alibi my friend. If something happens to me, my blood is on your hands. I thought we were brothers—I forgive you and I have asked that God forgives you for lying to the cops about me. Keep your mouth shut Barry.

Bar Jonah

* * *

After Cameron interviewed Barry, he drove back to his office. He hadn't yet sent off Bar Jonah's police jacket to the Montana Crime Lab for analysis. Things were piling up and he was starting to get behind. Cameron bagged up the jacket and sent it along with a letter to analyst Julie Long.

Dear Julie,

We have recovered a blue nylon police style jacket that we suspect Nathan Bar Jonah wore on the day he kidnapped Zachary Ramsay. We know that Bar Jonah brought the jacket to the dry cleaners several days after Zach Ramsay disappeared. We also know that the "side zipper" was replaced by the dry cleaners. All of this happened after Zachary Ramsay disappeared. The side zipper on this jacket has been replaced so it is the same jacket that he brought to the cleaners within days of Zachary disappearing. I don't know what type of testing can be done on this jacket since it was cleaned. I would like to know if some type of alternate light source or Luminal could be

190

used on the jacket to determine if there had been blood on the coat. Maybe there would still be a possibility of evidence lying under the zippered area after the repair. The jacket is dirty and does have some stains on it at this time. Any help you could give in regards to this matter would be greatly appreciated. Bar Jonah has 3 trials scheduled, the first being September 5, 2000. Although this jacket has now become part of the Zach Ramsay investigation, it was originally taken as evidence in an Impersonating an Officer case that goes to trial on September 5, 2000. The other piece of evidence I have enclosed is a piece of "meat or flesh" that was recovered from Bar Jonah's car. Is there a simple test to tell if this item is human? If so, I would like it tested. If the item is human I guess we can discuss several options. At this time we do not believe that the item would be related to the Zachary Ramsay investigation. The item could be related to the other remains that were found in Bar Jonah's garage. Thanks for all your help Julie. We continue to gather evidence and expect this investigation to go on for quite a long time. Unfortunately we have time constraints in the charges that Bar Jonah is already facing.

Respectfully,
Sgt. John A Cameron

After Cameron finished the letter he went out to the outgoing mail and dropped it into the worn cardboard box, sitting on the rickety table that should have been thrown out years before. When Cameron checked his in-box he found a letter from Mitotyping Technologies. He tore it open and went straight to the "Interpretation of Results." Cameron's heart sank, "The mtDNA in each of the questioned bone samples was determined to be degraded, which necessitated an "ancient DNA" analysis. The mitochondrial DNA sequences from the Q1, Q2, Q3, Q4, and Q5 bones and the KI blood (Rachel Howard's blood sample) do not match. Therefore, we can exclude the contributor(s) of these bone samples as a maternal relative of Rachel Howard." There was also a question in the mind of Dr Melton that the Q5 bone sample had been contaminated by *several* sources of DNA. Cameron walked back to the drying room where Wilson and Theisen were reading more of Bar Jonah's letters and announced the results. A sense of gloom filled the drying room like the piss mist in Doc's house.

CHAPTER TEN

Bridgewater and the metamorphosis

Digging through Bar Jonah's stacks of papers seemed never-ending. Theisen joked that Bar Jonah's crap reproduced each night after the lights were turned out. Cameron and Wilson peeled opened one of the dusty boxes and found that it was filled with stacks of Bar Jonah's prison records, including his past psychiatric evaluations dating back to the 1975 assault. Bar Jonah had even more reports than Bridgewater had bothered to send when Wilson had made his initial request. The first one that Cameron pulled out of the box was a psychological evaluation by Timothy Sinn, M.A., staff psychologist at Bridgewater.

> At the request of the department of mental health and in accordance with the provisions of section 9, chapter 123a, I conducted a psychiatric examination of David Brown at the Massachusetts treatment center. My examination consisted of two interviews on 8/18/83 and 8/25/83, as well as a review of his records at the treatment center. Prior to each interview I informed him as to who I was, the nature and purpose of the examination and the fact

that whatever was said was not confidential and could be used in my report. He indicated that he understood these conditions and agreed to talk with me. Mr. Brown is a 27-year-old single white male who was committed to the treatment center in June, 1979 following a conviction of attempted murder, and kidnapping of two young boys in 1977 for which he received 18–20 years. There has been at least one other similar previous offense for assault and battery on a young boy in which he disrobed him, choked him and then released him. While at the treatment center he has been quite resistant to treatment in any form. He had to be persuaded by other members in his large group to attend group in order not to lose his maximum tier privilege. His participation has been on the minimal side. He has the historical pattern of isolation and passivity, which is played out daily at the treatment center. He has rationalized his unwillingness to participate in group therapy because group therapy would not help him because his offenses are not sexual and he really doesn't belong here. His original willingness to come to the treatment center was because it seemed to be better than serving out a prison sentence. He has been seen by most of the staff as unable or unwilling to participate in therapy. In spite of his resistance to group and therapy he has allegedly been asking for an individual therapist for the past year.

It is not clear what his motivation is for this request. In fact, there is little that is clear regarding any of his motivations. He has no interpersonal relations, minimal job experience; medical defects of double vision, severe headaches, and blackouts, early sexual involvement with peer boys; aggressive assault on a peer girl; active fantasy life consisting of sadistic murderous ideations.

It appears that Mr. Brown's primary aim for these murderous assaults is the aggression, with sexual gratification being secondary. He is preoccupied with violence and unable to identify concurrent sexual feelings. However, he admits to experiencing erections when he thinks or does violent behaviors. Testing results indicate a very disturbed schizoid personality. Mr. Brown is an overweight individual who reports having high blood pressure when he was examined at Bridgewater State Hospital in 1977. He reports frequent "blurred," double and fuzzy vision since he was nine years old along with severe headaches "lasting up to nine days usually." Mr. Brown describes experiencing pounding in his head, which sometimes makes him cry. It should be noted Mr. Brown has one brown eye and one blue eye, which he states is a result of change when he was a baby ("It makes me different"). He has experienced blackouts "six of seven times" and suggests this may have happened during the current offense.

Timothy L. Sinn, Assistant Staff Psychologist

After Cameron read Sinn's report out loud, Wilson shook his head in disgust that not only Massachusetts but also Montana, in '94, had let Bar Jonah walk. The havoc that Bar Jonah had brought into the lives of children and their families made Wilson sick to his stomach.

Wilson reached into the box and pulled out another evaluation from Bridgewater, this one conducted by psychiatrist Robert Levy, M.D., from October 31st, 1983.

To The Presiding Justice
Worcester County Superior Court
Re: David Paul Brown, B.T. #407

Mr. Brown was able to trace back his assaultive behavior to 1963, when as a first grader, he suddenly began to strangle a female playmate. He reports that

195

he has read extensively about multiple murders, and has a long-standing interest in instruments of torture. His fantasies of violence have apparently been the predominant source of sexual excitement for him as he has had no adult heterosexual or homosexual experience. Mr. Brown is a large, almost massive individual weighing close to 375 pounds. His appearance is further notable because of one brown eye and one blue eye. He was able to relate in a comfortable, lucid and cooperative manner and displayed no evidence of either a thought disorder or other active psychotic process. He spoke quite openly about his awareness of the inner anger and rage he has inside of himself and articulated that he still has a lot left which will take a long time to come out. In addition he has some intellectual sense of the origins of this rage as well as the recognition that these feelings have become sexualized making them part of a private inner fantasy life that has been active for years. Mr. Brown also told me that his main purpose in filing this petition was to gain a better sense of what to work on. In this vein he spoke more than once of his persistent efforts to negotiate an individual treatment relationship. He seemed to acknowledge rather neutrally that he has not been able to reveal the kind of material that is therapeutically important in a group setting nor does he feel that this will change. He presents himself as clear that he wants and needs individual treatment and is tenacious in his efforts to obtain it, without being bitter or inappropriate.

I feel that Mr. Brown has made a good adjustment to the treatment center and recognizes that he will need many more years of (hopefully) individual treatment if he is to deal with and resolve the intense, sexualized rage that has led to his offenses and preoccupations with murder and torture. I would be inclined to support his request for an individual treatment relationship especially given the quality and nature of his inner world. At this time Mr. Brown remains a sexually dangerous person because he himself is only too aware of the inner anger and fantasies that continue to live within him. Without long-term treatment that would of necessity involve an important human relationship with a therapist(s), the likelihood of repeated offenses outside of the institution would be high.

Respectfully submitted
Robert D. Levy, M.D., Consultant Psychiatrist

It was clear that Bar Jonah had not been able to fool Sinn and Levy. They saw him as a "sexually dangerous person" and were concerned about his level of sexualized aggression. Each of the two evaluations Cameron and Wilson had looked at so far listed Bar Jonah's name as David Paul Brown. They knew that Bar Jonah had changed his name while he was in Bridgewater. What they didn't know at the time was how it had come about.

* * *

When he was first sent to Wapole State Penitentiary in 1977, he was nothing more than an isolated, fat, puerile baby-fucker, named David Paul Brown. It didn't take long before he discovered the world of prison pen pals. A network of lonely and frequently desperate people, men and women, looking for friends and sometimes, with more ominous consequences, men and women looking for mates. When David wrote letters, he hoped to get responses from women who were listed in one of the many lonely hearts publications that circulated throughout the prison. He was more often than not unsuccessful. His name was too ordinary. He had not yet begun to rehearse his epic myth about being raped by a gang of marauding neighborhood boys. For David this was a time of confusion and experimentation. He described himself as a chrysalis wanting to become a butterfly.

In August 1983, David began to think about changing his name. Within a few weeks, he had made his decision. Initially he thought about taking the name of "Job." His suffering had been so great, God had tested him, it only seemed right that he should inherit the mantle of the one that all other suffering is measured by. Since David had gone to prison, he had avoided and resisted almost all treatment, refusing individual and group psychotherapy and medications. But he did attend Bible study. Nothing would get in the way of David going to Bible study. On several occasions David had been disciplined after he dropped his Bible and photographs of young boys tumbled out onto the green scuffed tile floors: they were "distant cousins," he would argue.

* * *

When Tyra last visited him in August 1983, he told her that he had for sure decided to change his name. He no longer wanted to be known as David Brown. Tyra said she understood; he had to find his own path in life. Maybe changing his name would be a fresh start. Help him rid himself of the anguish of his tortured past. David told Tyra that he was going to take the name of "Job."

On the drive back up to Worchester, Tyra was ecstatic. At some point in time David would probably get out. God knows what he would do when he did. At least this way, she wouldn't have to bear the burden of being identified as his mother. Especially with the name of "Job." A few days later, Tyra got a letter in the mail. He had begun attending Jewish services at Bridgewater. It had made him realize that he wanted to become Jewish. After all, his religious heritage was Jewish, Tyra's maiden name being Bloomquist. He had decided to change his last name from Brown to Bloomquist. Tyra was furious. Rarely had she been so enraged at David. An hour after Tyra opened the letter, she was in her car speeding toward Bridgewater. She was there so many times during the week that the guards knew her by name. They were always so nice to bend the rules of visiting times. She could pretty much come and go as she pleased.

When she got out of the car, Tyra grabbed the crumpled letter she had received from David that was now laying crumpled on the passenger seat. As Tyra opened her car door, the acrid humid air came flooding over her. She was an old woman: the dense air made it harder and harder for her to get a good, long lasting breath. She waited for a moment, wiped the small beads of sweat from her forehead and struggled to pull herself out of the car. Before she closed the door, Tyra cranked the window a bit to let some of the heat escape while she was inside.

* * *

David's dull eyes lit up when he walked into the visitors lounge and unexpectedly saw Tyra. She was pacing around and around the green and soft pink Naugahyde chairs that were randomly spread throughout the room. When David walked toward Tyra, he noticed that her eyes were cold, aloof, and angry. As she paced, David saw his wrinkled letter scrunched up in her right hand. He walked over to her and wrapped his right arm around her shoulder and tried to pull her against him. Tyra was stiff as a board. She looked up at him, raised the crumpled letter to his face and said, "What is this crap about you taking my maiden name." David tried to explain that he wanted to explore his Jewish heritage. Tyra's voice crackled when she yelled, "We have no Jewish heritage, I am Swedish." In a rare stand of resistance against David's will Tyra told him flat out, "You will not use my maiden name and if you do I'll file a complaint against you in probate court." David bowed his head, dropped his chastised eyes and in an even rarer act of compliance, he immediately acquiesced. Tyra turned and began walking out of the visitors lounge. David stood stunned, listening to Tyra walking away, her tiny heels clicking one after the other against the tile floor, as she scurried toward the guard's station. She stopped suddenly, briefly turned around and said she was sorry but she was just so upset. The guard then heard her say, "How could you even think of doing this to my family."

* * *

Bar Jonah went back to his cell and prayed. He had been on the wrong path. The pain he had caused Tyra now made it clear to him that changing his name was not just a desire to be closer to his Jewish heritage, but a call from God to present himself to the world for who he was. David began studying his Bible more intensely and praying to the Lord God for guidance. In a few short nights, God came to David in his dreams. He was not only sure who he was in God's eyes, but he was now sure of the path that God had laid before him. The name he chose must reflect both. As with all his decisions, big and small, David began writing. Through God's guidance David was also sure that whatever name he chose, it must point more women with children in his direction. One thing that God had shown David through other inmates was that it was easier to be set free from Bridgewater's bondage if you had the open arms of a spouse-to-be waiting for you on the outside.

During the week of his realization, David barely left his cell. He had come to understand that there would be no discernment. He would not come to choose a name, a name would be chosen for him by the Lord. Everything was out of his control. He had to be patient and let the Lord's hand guide him. David was waking up in the middle of the night, not to the sound of clanging doors, but to the reverberations in his mind, after the Lord spoke to him through his dreams. He had been fervently reading his Bible day and night. For this week, he would give all to God, rarely even going to chow. This was bigger than he was. If he passed the test, God would surely reward him.

David was beginning to understand that he was one of the Lord's disciples, one of His chosen few. One who embodied the message of deliverance. Throughout his life David knew he had caused Tyra immense sorrow. He was sorry but Tyra had to understand that the Lord's plan for him was not a path without pain. Tyra, like the biblical Rachel, mother of Benjamin, must sacrifice herself if her son was to become who the Lord commanded him to be. Pain and suffering were the ways of Israelites. David remembered Deuteronomy 33:27: The eternal God is thy refuge, and underneath are the everlasting arms: and he shall thrust out the enemy from before thee; and shall say, Destroy them. The Lord had placed upon David many burdens, one of which was giving him keen powers of seeing the truth in all that he witnessed. This led to wisdom, perhaps the greatest burden of all. But through the granting of the gift of wisdom, David, like the Levites before him, of which he was a direct descendent, could now pass judgment. Two nights before he was ordained, David had another dream. A dream of Tamar. I am an Israeli soldier. I am fighting bravely and in the heat of battle I am wounded. My wounds are so bad that my leg must be amputated and I must use an artificial limb to get around. There is a nurse; she says her name is Tamar. Then David dreams the story of Tamar. She is a scared woman, a whore in the worst sense of the word. She tricks the good man Judah into making her pregnant while she's working as a whore in Enalm. For payment, Judah offers her a goat. She says no, she only wants the seal of his ring. Judah gives her the seal and goes on his way. Later he hears that a woman has given birth to twins. She is blaspheming the House of Judah with her lies, Judah decries. He orders her to be burnt to death. When Judah's slaves arrive to kill the woman, she says she has the seal of Judah and sends it back to Judah with his slaves. Judah is shamed and calls for the woman, who he knows as Tamar, to come and live in the House of Judah. But in all the time they are together, Judah will never have sex with her. He will never bring shame into his House again by defiling himself with Tamar. When David awakes, he knows that he must marry. He must find a wife. A wife who already has children

201

so he does not have to defile himself and bring shame upon his House.

* * *

David sat in his cell, wrapped in his rough wool blanket, having on nothing underneath, and opened his Bible. He could still feel himself running away from the Lord. He was trying to escape, as all prophets had, before the Lord caught up with them. And He always did. When David looked down at the open Bible lying on his lap, he realized that God had found him again. Like David, Jonah ben Amittai did not want to be a prophet. But God said it shall be so. But Jonah, like a disobedient child, ran away from the Lord, his God. Jonah tried to escape from the Lord by boarding a reed boat bound for Tarshish. The Lord was angry and made a violent storm rise up from the sea, causing Jonah to fall into the water. As he was falling, Jonah thought all was lost. He had angered the Lord and death was his punishment. Suddenly, Jonah was swallowed up by a great fish. A fish greater than any other fish had ever been. The Lord made Jonah spend three days and three nights inside the belly of the fish, before it came up out of the water and spat Jonah out onto the land. The Lord sent Jonah out to warn the people of Nineveh to repent, and they did. But Jonah was not pleased that he had fulfilled the command of the Lord. Jonah was angry. Throughout all of his life, Jonah would remain angry. He accepted the burden placed upon him by the Lord and ran away no more. But even the love of the Lord could never extinguish the fire that burned inside the belly of Jonah. David caressed the onion skin page and felt akin to Jonah.

* * *

David didn't dream that night. He had not tossed and turned on his bed either. Deep into the morning hours, David sat up, leaned back against the cinderblock wall, and opened his Bible again. The time had come. His name would be revealed to him

202

today. It was all there. He had kept copious notes; everything was written on his personal stationery. Stationery that would now need to be changed. When David shoved the covers to the end of the bed, he knocked his Bible onto the cold cement floor. The Good Book fell open to Leviticus, Chapter Seven. David knew Chapter Seven very well. It was one of his favorite books of the Bible. Before he reached down and picked up his Bible, David leaned back, deeply filled his lungs with the cool institutional morning air and exhaled for what seemed to be forever. He was filled with bliss. The Lord was with him now and forever. They were one. David scooted to the edge of the bed. He could feel his bulging belly fold itself in half, as he bent down to pick up his Bible. David than sat back and read Leviticus 7:1–9.

Right before David closed his Bible for the day and prepared to bring forth his name, he silently read one final passage from Leviticus. "This is the law of the burnt offering, of the meat offering, and of the sin offering, and of the trespass offering, and of the consecrations, and of the sacrifice of the peace offerings" (KJV, Leviticus 7:37). He made a few scribbles on a small white tablet and set it aside. David could feel the depth of the Lord when he pulled a long breath down to the bottom of his lungs. He held it for a moment, wanting to savor the fullness of God in His promise to him. Then he exhaled.

David pulled out a stack of papers from under his mattress and laid them out in chronological order from the first notations of his first realization to the notes he had just made. Then he picked up a loose piece of typing paper and a pencil that he regularly sharpened on the sharp edge of the underside of the metal frame of his bedsprings. He stopped before he went any further, looked up, and said, "To You oh Lord I commend My Spirit." Then David received his transformation from the Lord and wrote, "Nathaneal Benjamin Levi Bar Jonah" across the paper. He stood up and walked out of his cell and down to chow. He would never again be known as David Paul Brown.

As Nathaneal Benjamin Levi Bar Jonah sat down to eat, he began to write his first new ad for *Sweetheart* magazine. How was he going to describe himself? It came to him in a flash.

* * *

Cameron read to Wilson and Theisen, David Brown's account of how he became Bar Jonah. They sat transfixed. Cameron and Theisen were fascinated with the case. Wilson was fascinated with Bar Jonah. Anything Bar Jonah had written, Wilson was reading. From the tiniest scraps of paper to his voluminous, blue-lined spiral notebooks.

Wilson began to set Bar Jonah's writings out chronologically, looking at his earliest to his latest. There was so much that was written in some kind of code. The FBI cryptographers had begun to look at some of Bar Jonah's writings. One cryptographer told Wilson that he had never seen anyone, outside of Al Qaeda, write more in code than Bar Jonah. After many tries, the FBI was not able to fully unravel his code. It didn't fit any known scientific pattern and was more complex than any code they had ever seen. When the reports came back that Quantico was unable to crack the code, Wilson decided to take it on himself to try to do what he could to understand the sequencing of Bar Jonah's system of moving numbers and letters around. Even though Wilson had opened a file on the Ramsay case, it wasn't considered a high priority by the FBI, especially after four years of going nowhere. There wasn't a strong desire to put many more resources in it than they already had. This was a local matter: let them spend the money.

* * *

Cameron's marriage was now crumbling at a rapid pace. He was never home. The case had taken over his life. Theisen's wife, Laurie, continued to remain steadfast that Bar Jonah was not going to destroy their marriage. Wilson's marriage remained rock solid. The pressure from Groves never seemed to let up. Cameron and Theisen had to defend their work on the case day to day. Cameron would do anything that he could find to justify keeping the case alive. Groves battled him every step of the way. The biggest card Cameron had to draw on was of course that Zach Ramsay was still missing. In the five years since Zach had disappeared, the GFPD had made no progress in solving the case and for the most part had not put any resources into pursuing it. Cameron refused to let the case continue to falter. He knew he had Bar Jonah on the assault of the boys. But he as well as Wilson and Theisen wanted Bar Jonah for the murder of Zach. They were all dedicated to the final resolution of the case, however they hated going to work every day and dealing with the politics.

* * *

After Brown changed his name to Bar Jonah, responses to his ad in *Sweetheart* magazine dramatically increased. Before he changed his name, he was receiving about ten to twenty responses a month. Most of them were from single women, who didn't have children. Somehow the name David Brown didn't capture the imagination of many of the women scouring the magazine, seeking husbands. Within three months of changing his name, Bar Jonah was receiving more than 600 responses a month. His ad was catchy: "Roses are red, violets are blue, I'm marriage minded, you be too. I desire an already made family. I LOVE kids. I have tutti-fruity eyes, 5' 8" and weigh about 20 stones, have brown hair and have been known to be quite a character at times. I'm a gourmet cook. I LOVE to cook. Send $9.50 to help with my expenses." He was getting so many answers that he couldn't keep up by sending handwritten responses; Bar Jonah needed a computer.

* * *

Bar Jonah told Tyra that she had to make Bob get him a computer. It was the only way he could keep up with all his new pen pals. He was sure he was going to be able to find someone to marry through the ads he was placing. At some point, having a fiancée was going to help him get out of prison. Bob was a computer analyst and programmer. Bar Jonah told Tyra that a new computer, the Commodore 64, had just come out on the market. He wanted one. She and Bob could put their money together and get him one. They could afford it. Tyra tried to buck a bit, saying that she was living on a fixed income and that Lois and Bob had to help her out. Bar Jonah didn't care; they had a lot more money than he did and they weren't locked up. Bar Jonah issued an edict to Tyra: get him a computer or don't bother to come back and see him. He pointed out that Bob still had his first nickel. A few weeks later, a large package arrived at Bridgewater; Bar Jonah had got his Commodore 64. Bob even sent him a dot-matrix printer. The guards at Bridgewater were jealous and resentful. They didn't make much and couldn't afford something like that for their family. Yet Bar Jonah would now be sitting in his cell clicking out hundreds of letters a week and demanding that the guards take them to the mailroom immediately. Every Friday, Bar Jonah called Tyra collect, saying, "I want more stamps." He was meeting a lot of women who wanted to marry him; it was a big plus when they had kids. Bar Jonah said he wanted Tyra to be a grandmother to his kids. Just like the great mom she had always been to him. And, just as ordered, thick manila envelopes began arriving every Tuesday filled with stamps. Now Bar Jonah had all that he needed to offer himself up to those struggling mothers who'd been left by their men to bring their boys up right and fend for themselves. He was ready for his mission. It was the Lord's will and His work.

It would prove to be a very long time before that work were brought to an end.

NOTES

Adams, D., personal communication, July, 2009
Bar Jonah, N., personal communication, January, 2002–May, 2002
Beljan, P., personal communication, January, 2002–May, 2002
Bellusci, W., personal communication, June, 2009
Brown, R., personal communication, April, 2002
Brown, T., personal communication, April, 2002
Cameron, J., personal communication, April, 2009–December, 2011
Flaherty, P., personal communication, July, 2009
Gustovich, D., personal communication, August, 2009
Hipskind, G., personal communication, June, 2009
Howard, R., personal communication, May, 2009–June, 2010
Howard, S., personal communication, October, 2009
Kimmerle, D., personal communication, August, 2009
Light, B., personal communication, April, 2009–12 June, 2012
Metzger, M., personal communication, July, 2009
Patterson, R., personal communication, June, 2009–August, 2009
Perkins, M., personal communication, August, 2010–November, 2011
Richardson, M., personal communication, August, 2009
Scott, L., personal communication, July, 2009
Spamer, B., personal communication, August, 2010–June, 2012
Theisen, T., personal communication, April, 2009–December, 2012
Wilson, J., personal communication, June, 2009

All trial related material is taken verbatim from trial transcripts or
court related material in the public domain.
All poetry by Bar Jonah is a matter of public record.

REFERENCES

Belkin, D. (2000). Cops seek other child victims in cannibal case / City horrified by alleged cannibal case / Boy, 5, may have been served to neighbors. *Boston Globe*, 31 December, p. 1. Available at: www.sfgate.com/news/article/Cops-Seek-Other-Child-Victims-in-Cannibal-Case-2718264.php#ixzz2HD9zrJLl.

Bruck, M., & Ceci, S. (1993). Child witnesses: Translating research into policy. *Social Policy Report*, 7(3), Fall.

Dracula Has Risen from the Grave (1968). Dir. Freddie Francis. Perf. Christopher Lee, Rupert Davies, Hammer Film Productions.

Great Falls Tribune (1991). Letter testifying to the miracles of Jesus Christ. November.

Hamblen, S. (1954). *This Ole House*, released by EMI on the His Master's Voice label as catalogue numbers B 10761 and 7M 269.

Interview with Bar Jonah (2005). Missing Children International Ministry. July.

In the Name of Jesus All Things Are Possible (1749). Charles Wesley, Hymns and Sacred Poems, Volume II. http://www.hymntime.com/tch/htm/a/l/l/allthings.htm.

The Texas Chainsaw Massacre (1974). Dir. Tobe Hooper. Perf. Marilyn Burns, Edwin Neal, Vortex Films.

ABOUT THE AUTHOR

John C. Espy, PhD, LCSW, has been practicing psychotherapy and psychoanalysis for the past thirty-five years. He was supervised by R. D. Laing for many years and conducted a weekly supervision group with Sheldon Kopp. He has worked extensively in the area of primitive and psychotic personalities and has interviewed more than twenty serial murderers and pedophiles in the United States and Europe as part of his research on the manifestation of malignant projective-identification. His current practice primarily focuses on clinical and forensic consultation and long-term treatment. He was previously a neurotoxicologist with NASA and has taught at numerous universities throughout the United States. Dr. Espy is also a long-standing member of the American Academy of Psychotherapists, the American Association for Psychoanalysis in Clinical Social Work, and northwestern United States group moderator for the International Neuropsychoanalysis Society.